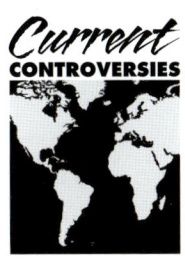

The Capitol Riot
Fragile Democracy

Other Books in the Current Controversies Series

Attacks on Science
Big Tech and Democracy
Cyberterrorism
Domestic Extremism
Domestic vs. Offshore Manufacturing
Fossil Fuel Industries and the Green Economy
Hate Groups
The Internet of Things
Libertarians, Socialists, and Other Third Parties
The Politics and Science of COVID-19
Reparations for Black Americans
Sustainable Consumption

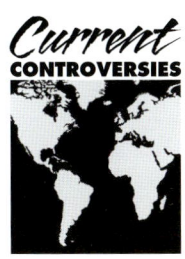

The Capitol Riot
Fragile Democracy

Gary Wiener, Book Editor

Published in 2022 by Greenhaven Publishing, LLC
353 3rd Avenue, Suite 255, New York, NY 10010

Copyright © 2022 by Greenhaven Publishing, LLC

First Edition

All rights reserved. No part of this book may be reproduced in any form without permission in writing from the publisher, except by a reviewer.

Articles in Greenhaven Publishing anthologies are often edited for length to meet page requirements. In addition, original titles of these works are changed to clearly present the main thesis and to explicitly indicate the author's opinion. Every effort is made to ensure that Greenhaven Publishing accurately reflects the original intent of the authors. Every effort has been made to trace the owners of the copyrighted material.

Cover image: lev radin/Shutterstock.com

Library of Congress CataloginginPublication Data

Names: Wiener, Gary, editor.
Title: The Capitol Riot : fragile democracy / Gary Wiener, book editor.
Description: First edition. | New York, NY : Greenhaven Publishing, 2022. | Series: Current controversies | Includes bibliographical references and index. | Audience: Ages 15+ | Audience: Grades 10-12 | Summary: "Anthology of diverse perspectives addressing the conditions that allowed the January 6, 2021, insurrection at the US Capitol and what it means for democracy"-- Provided by publisher.
Identifiers: LCCN 2021029615 | ISBN 9781534508590 (library binding) | ISBN 9781534508583 (paperback) | ISBN 9781534508606 (ebook)
Subjects: LCSH: Capitol Riot, Washington, D.C., 2021--Juvenile literature. | Political violence--Washington (D.C.)--Juvenile literature. | Presidents--United States--Election--2020. | Contested elections--United States--Juvenile literature. | Democracy--United States--Juvenile literature. | Domestic terrorism--United States--Juvenile literature. | Demonstrations--Washington (D.C.)--Juvenile literature.
Classification: LCC E915 .C37 2022 | DDC 973.933--dc23
LC record available at https://lccn.loc.gov/2021029615

Manufactured in the United States of America

Website: http://greenhavenpublishing.com

Contents

Foreword   11
Introduction   14

Chapter 1: Were the Capitol Rioters Truly Protesting the Results of the Presidential Election?

Overview: Some Americans Don't Believe the Election Results   19
David M. Mayer

The outcome of the 2020 presidential election was central to many citizens' sense of identity. This personal setback caused skepticism regarding the election results. It is important for elected leaders to validate the electoral process in order to quell the doubts of those who are dubious about the outcome.

Yes: The Rioters Would Not Accept the Election Results

Trump's Claims About the Fraudulent Election Stirred Up His Base   23
Lori Robertson, Jessica McDonald, Robert Farley, D'Angelo Gore, and Rem Rieder

The facts garnered from swing states convincingly upheld the notion of a secure election. Even though accusations of voter fraud in these states have been thoroughly vetted and debunked, Trump voters had a hard time conceding.

Trump Loyalists Would Not See That Joe Biden's Victory Was Indisputable   36
Lily Hay Newman

While voter fraud does occur in rare instances, there is no evidence that the Democrats systematically conspired to steal the election by using coronavirus as an excuse for mail-in voting or by otherwise gaming the system.

Claims of Voter Fraud Have a Long History in America   44
David Litt

False claims of voter fraud are not isolated to the 2020 presidential election. It is a time-honored, if unethical, political strategy: in a best-case scenario it can be used to disenfranchise voters in an election that already occurred, and in a worse-case scenario it lays the groundwork for disenfranchising them the next time.

No: There Was More Behind the Insurrection Than the Election

January 6 Brought Trump to a True Level of Fascism   48
Paul Nicholas Jackson

Leading academics weigh in on the debate over whether Donald Trump is a fascist. The unprecedented events of January 6, 2021, put many experts over the edge in confidently affixing that label to the former president.

A Strain of Nihilism Infected Trump and the MAGA Movement   67
Ani Kokobobo

The author uses Russian novelist Fyodor Dostoevsky's work to predict the worst case scenario for American society in the wake of the Capitol riot. Dostoevsky explored the effect on a society when its leaders lack moral convictions and find no meaning in society. Does the MAGA movement fit such a scenario?

QAnon Arose to Meet Trump's Conspiratorial Needs   71
Ethan Zuckerman

The author delves into how the conspiracist community surrounding QAnon represents a hazardous new form of participatory civics and digital storytelling.

Chapter 2: Was Donald Trump Responsible for the Capitol Riot?

Overview: What Trump Said Before the Capitol Riot   89
Amy Sherman

President Donald Trump's own words prior to and during the Capitol riot are laid out so that readers can judge for themselves whether he was complicit in stoking the insurrection.

Yes: Donald Trump Was Primarily Responsible for the January 6th Riot at the Capitol

Trump's Supporters Undermine His Impeachment Defense   94
Zoe Tillman

During the second impeachment trial of Donald Trump, the words of his own supporters were cited as proof that Trump himself was responsible for the Capitol riot on January 6, 2021.

Trump's Own Words and Lack of Action Show Responsibility — 98

Diane Ravitch

The president may not have understood what he'd done when he implored protesters to march to the Capitol, but his reluctance as chief executive of the United States to call off the angry mob once they'd begun their riot leaves no question as to his part in the insurrection.

No: Numerous Other Factors Led to the Capitol Riot

Social Media Bears Some of the Blame for the Riot — 106

Erika D. Smith

The Capitol riot was the inevitable and ugly outcome of social media companies leaving conspiracy theories to fester and spread lies and threats of violence online.

Ex-Delaware Attorney General Says Trump Is Not Responsible for Capitol Siege — 110

Meredith Newman, Ryan Cormier, and Sarah Gamard

According to Republicans, Trump faced unprecedented attacks from the political left during the course of his presidency. It was no wonder, therefore, that his supporters were angry and took out their frustrations on January 6.

Chapter 3: Should Those Who Stormed the Capitol Be Harshly Punished?

Overview: The Capitol Riots Provided America with a Teachable Moment — 116

Scott Shackford

It is dangerous to respond to emotion-driven criminal behavior with emotion-driven legal enforcement. But the rioters need to understand the severity of their behavior and that it was the prior work of criminal justice reformers that will ultimately result in their being given a just form of punishment.

Yes: The Capitol Rioters Committed Serious Crimes and Must Be Held Responsible

Most Americans Want the Rioters Prosecuted — 122
Pew Research Center

According to a Pew Research poll, an overwhelming majority of Americans want the rioters to be punished for their crimes. Predictably, opinions often break along party lines.

The Capitol Was Invaded Because of a Failure to Punish Those Who Had Attacked State Capitols — 133
Jeremy Kohler

Before the rioters invaded the United States Capitol, right wing groups had already brazenly stormed several state capitol buildings with impunity. The lack of consequences for these trespassers emboldened them and led directly to the January 6th riot.

Congress Must Defend the Constitution — 139
Niskanen Center

It appears that some Republican members of Congress did more than amplify destabilizing election falsehoods. Some may have actively planned to bring a mob to the Capitol steps with the intent of influencing the electoral count. If true, they should be removed from Congress and face criminal prosecution.

No: The Rioters Were Pawns in the System and Others Are Equally Guilty

Restraint Must Be Used When Considering Harsh Punishments for the Capitol Rioters — 144
Eric Westervelt

An interview with former FBI agent Andy Arena argues that prosecutors must be measured in their response to the Capitol riots. Levelling sedition charges is not likely to succeed and could boomerang on future protesters and stifle legitimate dissent.

The Capitol Rioters Believe That Trump Owed Them Pardons — 148
Kevin Rector and Chris Megarian

Speaking through their defense lawyers or in interviews, the Capitol rioters insisted they did nothing illegal. They couldn't have been trespassing, they argue, because they entered the Capitol at the "invitation" of President Trump and were following his direct orders.

Why Should the Rioters Be Punished and Not Their Enablers?   **152**

Julie Erfle

The rioters deserve whatever punishment they receive, but those who encouraged them also deserve to be prosecuted. The elected officials, media outlets, and corporate executives who profited from years of chaos and division are just as guilty.

Chapter 4: Did the Riot Endanger Democracy?

Overview: Was the Capitol Riot a Coup Attempt?   **157**

Clayton Besaw and Matthew Frank

While the January 6 riot was an example of election violence that plagues many countries, it did not quite rise to the level of a coup, which can be defined as an attempt by the military or other elites within the state apparatus to unseat the sitting head of state using unconstitutional means.

Yes: America Faces a Systemic Collapse into Authoritarianism

Most Voters Say the Capitol Riot Threatened Democracy   **161**

Matthew Smith, Jamie Ballard, and Linley Sanders

Though a large majority of voters believes that the Capitol riot was a danger to America's democratic system, responders were divided along party lines.

Young People Worry About the Future of America in the Wake of the Capitol Riot   **164**

Artea Brahaj, Hannah J. Martinez, and Meimei Xu

Young people were largely shocked and appalled by the goings-on at the US Capitol. The riot has caused many to fear for the future of America.

World Leaders Were Appalled by the Storming of the US Capitol   **168**

Anthony Galloway

Leaders around the world viewed the Capitol riot with shock and awe. Even leaders of undemocratic countries were surprised by the insurrection in Washington. Some saw the opportunity to gloat, while others hoped for the quick restoration of the democratic process in a country torn apart by political divisions.

No: Democracy Will Survive the Capitol Riot

American Democracy Has Once Again Survived   172
Bo Rothstein
If elected leaders do not take a stand against political violence, do not respect the democratic rights of their opponents, and refrain from promising to respect an election result that goes against them, then democracy is in danger. Ultimately, American democracy was saved by two principles: impartiality in the implementation of public policies and knowledge realism.

We Need to Address the Insurrection's Root Causes   176
Maria J. Stephan
To prevent future far-right violence, first we need accountability. Then we must build movements capable of transforming our social, political, and economic systems.

Despite the Flagrant Assault on the Capitol, the Pillars of Democracy Are Holding   183
Eileen Flanagan
A coup needs legitimacy to be successful. If the goal of seizing the Capitol was to gain legitimacy, the action backfired spectacularly.

Organizations to Contact   188
Bibliography   193
Index   197

Foreword

"Controversy" is a word that has an undeniably unpleasant connotation. It carries a definite negative charge. Controversy can spoil family gatherings, spread a chill around classroom and campus discussion, inflame public discourse, open raw civic wounds, and lead to the ouster of public officials. We often feel that controversy is almost akin to bad manners, a rude and shocking eruption of that which must not be spoken or thought of in polite, tightly guarded society. To avoid controversy, to quell controversy, is often seen as a public good, a victory for etiquette, perhaps even a moral or ethical imperative.

Yet the studious, deliberate avoidance of controversy is also a whitewashing, a denial, a death threat to democracy. It is a false sterilizing and sanitizing and superficial ordering of the messy, ragged, chaotic, at times ugly processes by which a healthy democracy identifies and confronts challenges, engages in passionate debate about appropriate approaches and solutions, and arrives at something like a consensus and a broadly accepted and supported way forward. Controversy is the megaphone, the speaker's corner, the public square through which the citizenry finds and uses its voice. Controversy is the life's blood of our democracy and absolutely essential to the vibrant health of our society.

Our present age is certainly no stranger to controversy. We are consumed by fierce debates about technology, privacy, political correctness, poverty, violence, crime and policing, guns, immigration, civil and human rights, terrorism, militarism, environmental protection, and gender and racial equality. Loudly competing voices are raised every day, shouting opposing opinions, putting forth competing agendas, and summoning starkly different visions of a utopian or dystopian future. Often these voices attempt to shout the others down; there is precious little listening and considering among the cacophonous din. Yet listening and considering, too, are essential to the health of a democracy. If controversy is democracy's lusty lifeblood, respectful listening and careful thought are its higher faculties, its brain, its conscience.

Current Controversies does not shy away from or attempt to hush the loudly competing voices. It seeks to provide readers with as wide and representative as possible a range of articulate voices on any given controversy of the day, separates each one out to allow it to be heard clearly and fairly, and encourages careful listening to each of these well-crafted, thoughtfully expressed opinions, supplied by some of today's leading academics, thinkers, analysts, politicians, policy makers, economists, activists, change agents, and advocates. Only after listening to a wide range of opinions on an issue, evaluating the strengths and weaknesses of each argument, assessing how well the facts and available evidence mesh with the stated opinions and conclusions, and thoughtfully and critically examining one's own beliefs and conscience can the reader begin to arrive at his or her own conclusions and articulate his or her own stance on the spotlighted controversy.

This process is facilitated and supported in each Current Controversies volume by an introduction and chapter overviews that provide readers with the essential context they need to begin engaging with the spotlighted controversies, with the debates surrounding them, and with their own perhaps shifting or nascent opinions on them. Chapters are organized around several key questions that are answered with diverse opinions representing all points on the political spectrum. In its content, organization, and methodology, readers are encouraged to determine the authors' point of view and purpose, interrogate and analyze the various arguments and their rhetoric and structure, evaluate the arguments' strengths and weaknesses, test their claims against available facts and evidence, judge the validity of the reasoning, and bring into clearer, sharper focus the reader's own beliefs and conclusions and how they may differ from or align with those in the collection or those of classmates.

Foreword

Research has shown that reading comprehension skills improve dramatically when students are provided with compelling, intriguing, and relevant "discussable" texts. The subject matter of these collections could not be more compelling, intriguing, or urgently relevant to today's students and the world they are poised to inherit. The anthologized articles also provide the basis for stimulating, lively, and passionate classroom debates. Students who are compelled to anticipate objections to their own argument and identify the flaws in those of an opponent read more carefully, think more critically, and steep themselves in relevant context, facts, and information more thoroughly. In short, using discussable text of the kind provided by every single volume in the Current Controversies series encourages close reading, facilitates reading comprehension, fosters research, strengthens critical thinking, and greatly enlivens and energizes classroom discussion and participation. The entire learning process is deepened, extended, and strengthened.

If we are to foster a knowledgeable, responsible, active, and engaged citizenry, we must provide readers with the intellectual, interpretive, and critical-thinking tools and experience necessary to make sense of the world around them and of the all-important debates and arguments that inform it. We must encourage them not to run away from or attempt to quell controversy but to embrace it in a responsible, conscientious, and thoughtful way, to sharpen and strengthen their own informed opinions by listening to and critically analyzing those of others. This series encourages respectful engagement with and analysis of current controversies and competing opinions and fosters a resulting increase in the strength and rigor of one's own opinions and stances. As such, it helps readers assume their rightful place in the public square and provides them with the skills necessary to uphold their awesome responsibility—guaranteeing the continued and future health of a vital, vibrant, and free democracy.

Introduction

> "For decades ... the US was able to promote democracy based on its own example: a stable system in which power has been passed peacefully for some 220 years ... Trump's incitement of a mob of supporters which stormed the Capitol not only broke that chain of hitherto peaceful transfers of power, it showed the world that the US is no different than the countries it had admonished in the past."[1]

"Stop the Steal!" These words became the mantra of President Donald Trump's supporters once it became clear that former vice president Joe Biden would win the 2020 presidential election. The slogan was concocted by Trump associate and self-described conservative dirty trickster Roger Stone, a man who had been dipping his hands into the mud puddle of politics since the Nixon era. Stone is also a convicted felon whose prison sojourn was avoided only by Trump's commutation of his sentence. Though the Stop the Steal campaign might have seemed to emerge organically on the internet, Stone had already begun using it to raise money as far back as 2016 during Trump's first campaign, when Trump's camp worried that other Republicans might wrest the party's presidential nomination away from the man they fondly referred to as the Donald.

So the stage had been set for Trump to decry voter fraud long before November 4, 2020. Because the country was so radically divided and the rhetoric of the race so heated, and because conservatives had a four-year history of ignoring Trump's daily statements, those on the right, and especially those on the far right, readily accepted the stolen election theory as received fact. And on January 6, 2021, as Congress was convening at the Capitol to certify the results of the November election, thousands of Trump supporters flooded Washington with the intent of letting their elected representatives know just how disenchanted they were with the electoral process.

The resulting violence was predictable, given that many of these self-proclaimed patriots were members of far-right militias and assorted hate groups. What may have begun as a peaceful protest coordinated by Trump himself and associates such as former New York City mayor Rudy Giuliani, quickly devolved into chaos. All across the country, and the world, those watching the news on that fateful January 6 were horrified by the violent images that appeared on their television screens.

Rioters fought with Capitol police officers. They breeched the Capitol and smashed windows. They trespassed into the building itself, shouting threats such as "Hang [Vice President] Mike Pence." They vandalized congressional offices and stole congressional property, causing an estimated 1.5 million dollars in damage. And, most significant, they delayed, if only for hours, the certification of Joe Biden as the forty-sixth president of the United States.

Although Trump had assured the protesters that he would march with them to the Capitol building, he did not. From the safety of the White House, the forty-fifth president viewed the insurrection on television.

Despite calls from members of Congress, Trump was loathe to interfere with the rioters. He and the House minority leader, Republican Kevin McCarthy, exchanged an expletive-laden phone call during which Trump refused to send additional forces to suppress the riot. "Well, Kevin, I guess these people are more upset about the election than you are," Trump said, according to lawmakers who were briefed on the call afterward by McCarthy. "[Trump] is not a blameless observer. He was rooting for them," a Republican member of Congress said.

When Trump finally did issue a statement, he asked the rioters to "go home in peace." But those words came long after the riot had reached critical mass. Ultimately, five people died during the attack on the Capitol, including a Capitol police officer, Brian Sicknick. Hundreds were wounded. Two Capitol police officers committed suicide in the aftermath of the attack. To this day, many are being treated for PTSD.

January 6, 2021, will continue to be a blemish on the United States. The country has been a bastion of democracy in the world's eyes, a "city on a hill" upon which the rest of the planet could gaze with admiration and respect. Leaders of democracies around the globe were shocked, and many horrified, by what they witnessed on that January day. Some authoritarians reacted with *schadenfreude*, suggesting that the United States was not so high and mighty anymore, and that it would be hypocritical if our leaders criticized other countries about their shady election practices. Russian President Vladimir Putin mocked the riot as a "stroll" while gloating about dysfunction in the US government.

Whatever one's political beliefs, it is safe to say that the attack on the US Capitol was not America's finest moment. As a result of the riot, outgoing president Trump was impeached by the House of Representatives for a second time. More than five hundred of those who breeched the Capitol building are now facing charges. And American democracy is arguably hovering on the brink.

In the aftermath of January 6, Republican lawmakers shot down a Democratic-led initiative to launch an investigative commission. Trump himself sent out missives that assured his followers he would be "reinstated" to the presidency. Exactly what that would entail is unclear, for the US Constitution contains no language about such an occurrence. The one thing that is certain about the Capitol riot is that it will affect US politics for years to come. It is likely to become a seminal date in American history alongside 9/11 and December 7, 1941. In *Current Controversies: The Capitol Riot*, a wide range of experts debate the issues surrounding the attack and its reflection on the state of democracy, providing an insightful and though-provoking range of opinions.

Notes

1. "The Capitol Riots Showed US Democracy's Vulnerability. How Does That Affect Its Global Influence?" by Wilson Liévano and Josh Coe, The Groundtruth Project, January 15, 2021.

Chapter 1

Were the Capitol Rioters Truly Protesting the Results of the Presidential Election?

Overview: Some Americans Don't Believe the Election Results

David M. Mayer

David M. Mayer is a professor in the management and organizations area at the Ross School of Business at the University Michigan. An award-winning researcher and highly rated and sought-after teacher and speaker, he is an expert on helping people and organizations lead ethically, inclusively, and positively.

The electoral votes have confirmed Joe Biden won the 2020 United States presidential election. The presidential electors gave Biden 306 electoral votes to President Donald Trump's 232 votes. Biden also recorded a solid lead of over 7 million in the popular vote.

Nonetheless, results from a new NPR/PBS NewsHour/Marist survey found that approximately three-quarters of Republicans did not trust the election results. Corroborating this finding, a separate study of 24,000 Americans found that nearly two-thirds of Republicans lacked confidence in the fairness of the election and over 80% feared fraud, inaccuracy, bias and illegality. In addition, nearly 60 lawsuits filed by Trump claiming various forms of election fraud have been dismissed, including two evaluated by the US Supreme Court.

Of course, doubting the fairness of a disappointing decision is not a Republican phenomenon—it's a human one.

When a decision is made and people get the outcome they want, they often tend to see the outcome as fair. For example, when people apply for a promotion and get it, they are more than likely to believe they deserved it. But if they didn't get the promotion, it is likely to drive a different reaction. At that point, the process used

"The Psychology of Fairness: Why Some Americans Don't Believe the Election Results," by David M. Mayer, The Conversation, December 21, 2020. https://theconversation.com/the-psychology-of-fairness-why-some-americans-dont-believe-the-election-results-152305. Licensed under CC BY-ND 4.0.

to make the decision becomes of utmost importance. Some might ask whether the process was free of bias, consistent and ethical.

To investigate this perplexing phenomenon, it's important to understand the psychology of fairness.

Fair Procedures Usually Matter

Research consistently finds that when people get an unfavorable outcome but believe the process used to make the decision was fair, they react more positively.

They may be disappointed, but they tend to accept the decision and stay loyal to the institution that made the decision. This is known as the "fair process effect": the tendency for fair procedures to mitigate negative reactions to an unfavorable decision.

However, research my colleagues and I conducted in 2009 identifies an important caveat to this effect. We found that when an unfavorable decision is very important to someone—that it is central to their identity as part of a group or their personal values—they tend to look for flaws demonstrating that the process used to make the decision was unfair.

In the first study, we asked 180 university students about a decision that the administration would soon make about limiting the free speech of students. We manipulated whether the outcome was favorable such that half of the students were told the administration planned to restrict free speech and the other half were told there would be no restrictions. We also manipulated the process by telling students they had an opportunity to express their concerns in a public forum or did not have that opportunity.

We then assessed whether the decision made by the administration violated students' identity as a member of the university and their personal values.

We found that when students felt the decision violated their social or personal identity, they perceived the process and outcome were unfair even when they had the opportunity to express their views at a public forum. In other words, there was a weak or no relationship between providing an opportunity for voice and fairness perceptions for people whose identity was violated.

In the second study we asked 277 adults with work experience about a time a decision was made at work when the outcome was favorable (or not) and the process was fair (or not).

As in the prior study, we found that an objectively fair process did not improve fairness perceptions when an outcome violated one's identity. Instead, these participants were more likely to say that there was a procedural flaw—they doubted the opinions they provided to the decision-maker were ever considered.

The fact that they did not get the outcome they wanted on something that was central to their identity led participants to seek out reasons that an objectively fair process was somehow flawed in a meaningful way. They felt the need to discredit the process.

These findings are consistent with other research showing that for those who have a strong moral stance on an issue, judgments about whether the process and outcome are fair are determined more by whether the outcome was favorable than whether the procedure was objectively fair.

For example, when participants supported abortion rights, and a defendant in a trial was not convicted of bombing a clinic that performed abortions, these participants believed the trial process was less fair than those who held anti-abortion rights beliefs.

Similarly, when participants held anti-abortion rights beliefs and a physician on trial for providing illegal late-term abortions was acquitted, participants believed the trial was less fair than did those with abortion-rights beliefs. When we care deeply about an issue and get an unfavorable outcome, we question the process used to make the decision.

What Can You Do?

In an environment in which partisan and identity politics rule, perhaps it is not surprising that a decision that hurts one's in-group—in this case, Republican supporters—is dismissed on the basis of perceived procedural flaws that render the election unfair despite objective reality.

Of course, the act of discounting the fairness of a decision process when a decision violates one's identity is not limited to one political party. For example, after Brett Kavanaugh was confirmed as a Supreme Court justice, Democrats tended to believe that his confirmation hearings were unjust, including the withholding of important evidence.

Given that anyone can fall victim to this bias, several things can be done. First, it is important for leaders to legitimize the decision process. For example, when an organization makes a policy change to extend or reduce the number of remote days of work per week, it is important for leadership at all levels to clarify there was reasonable and fair process used to make the decision.

Second, it is critical to ask someone who is impartial. When wrestling with an ethical conundrum, people often come to a conclusion that is aligned with their self-interest—what psychologists call "motivated moral reasoning." Thus, a neutral person can more accurately assess the decision.

Third, reducing how much a person feels distinct and isolated from members of another group by not dehumanizing members of the other group can lessen beliefs that a decision process was rigged or biased.

People often do not get the outcome they want on issues central to their identity, so it is important to actively guard against questioning the legitimacy of an objective and fair process.

Trump's Claims About the Fraudulent Election Stirred Up His Base

Lori Robertson, Jessica McDonald, Robert Farley, D'Angelo Gore, and Rem Rieder

Lori Robertson, Jessica McDonald, Robert Farley, D'Angelo Gore, and Rem Rieder write for Factcheck.org, a nonpartisan, nonprofit consumer advocate for voters that aims to reduce the level of deception and confusion in US politics. Robertson is managing editor. McDonald writes mainly about science. Farley is deputy managing editor. Gore is a staff writer, and Rieder is a former senior writer and editor at large.

In remarks resembling an attack on democratic elections, rather than a presidential speech, President Donald Trump doubled down on his campaign pledge: "The only way we can lose, in my opinion, is massive fraud."

In his Nov. 5 comments, he offered no evidence for the "illegal votes" that he claimed would need to be counted in order for former Vice President Joe Biden to win the election. He offered several false, misleading and baseless claims instead.

We'll go through Trump's claims about voting in several states, beginning with Pennsylvania.

[…]

Pennsylvania

In speaking about the Keystone State, Trump baselessly alleged election engineering and mischaracterized a court ruling related to partisan election observers. While one ruling allowed observers to get as close as 6 feet, the president's claim that "they don't want

"Trump's Wild, Baseless Claims of Illegal Voting," by Lori Robertson, Jessica McDonald, Robert Farley, D'Angelo Gore, and Rem Rieder, November 6, 2020. Copyright © 2020 by FactCheck.org, a project of the Annenberg Public Policy Center Reprinted by permission..

us to have any observers" is false. There is also no evidence that local officials have improperly handled the election.

"We were up by nearly 700,000 votes in Pennsylvania. I won Pennsylvania by a lot. And that gets whittled down to, I think they said now we're up by 90,000 votes and they'll keep coming and coming and coming," Trump said. "They find them all over and they don't want us to have any observers. Although we won a court case, the judge said, 'You have to have observers.'"

As we've explained before, Trump cannot claim to have won Pennsylvania. The earlier vote returns were in his favor, as the in-person votes were counted more quickly, but mail-in and absentee ballots could not even be opened and prepared for counting until 7 a.m. on Nov. 3. The count of legitimately cast ballots is still proceeding.

Because more Democrats tended to vote by mail—likely due, in part, to the party's active encouragement of such ballots to lock in votes early—many more of the votes that were counted later were for Biden, leading to a "blue shift" over time. Democrats accounted for nearly two-thirds of the 2.6 million returned mail-in ballots, according to an analysis of Pennsylvania election data by Michael McDonald, a University of Florida political science professor who maintains the US Elections Project.

And indeed, as many analysts expected, the Democratic nominee took the lead in the state on the morning of Nov. 6.

Trump also baselessly said that Philadelphia was in the process of "engineering the outcome of a presidential race" and that "officials overseeing the counting in Pennsylvania and other key states are all part of a corrupt Democrat machine."

There's no indication that any election malfeasance has occurred. It's also not true that all of the officials in charge of counting ballots are Democrats. In Philadelphia, that job falls to a bipartisan trio of commissioners that includes one Republican.

The commonwealth's website similarly states that "bipartisan teams of election officials in each county are making sure your vote is accurately counted and verified."

Trump then proceeded to mischaracterize litigation pertaining to observers watching the vote counting process, saying that Democrats "have gone to the state Supreme Court to try and ban our election observers and very strongly."

The dispute has been over how close observers can get to the canvassing proceedings, not whether observers are allowed to be present. Initially, a trial court denied the Trump campaign's request for closer observation in Philadelphia, finding on Nov. 3 that by the campaign's own admission, it had been given the opportunity to observe "the opening and sorting of ballots."

The next day, a state court reversed that ruling, allowing observers within 6 feet, "while adhering to all COVID-19 protocols, including, wearing masks and maintaining social distancing." Philadelphia's election board then appealed the ruling to the state Supreme Court, saying that it had complied with the law and that closer inspection "jeopardizes both the safety of the City Defendants' canvass, plus the privacy of voters."

Separately, but on the same issue, the Trump campaign filed suit in federal court on Nov. 5 to stop the vote count in Philadelphia. That request was dismissed by a judge—who was appointed by President George W. Bush—after both sides agreed that each would be allowed 60 observers. The Trump lawyer admitted during the hearing that the campaign did have some canvassing observers present, stating, "There's a non-zero number of people in the room."

Philadelphia, notably, has been livestreaming its vote canvassing, which is available online for anyone to watch.

Trump also misleadingly summarized a previous state Supreme Court decision that permits ballots that are postmarked by Nov. 3 to be accepted if received by Nov. 6. (In refusing a Republican request to expedite review of the case, the US Supreme Court let the state court decision stand—but could opt to revisit the case after the election.)

"In Pennsylvania, partisan Democrats have allowed ballots in the state to be received three days after the election, and we think much more than that, and they're counting those without even postmarks or any identification whatsoever," he said. "So you don't have postmarks, you don't have identification."

According to the rules, which were implemented due to concerns about postal delays during the COVID-19 pandemic, a ballot postmarked by Election Day can be accepted if received by 5 p.m. on Nov. 6. In the rare case in which there is a missing or illegible postmark, ballots without postmarks will be allowed unless there is a "preponderance of evidence" they were mailed after the deadline.

Pennsylvania Secretary of the Commonwealth Kathy Boockvar explained in a Nov. 4 press conference that the vast majority of these later-arriving ballots should have postmarks on them, as that is standard fare for mail. Trump, therefore, is wrong to suggest that most or all of these ballots would not have postmarks.

It's also false for the president to claim that the ballots do not require "any identification whatsoever." According to the state's website, "In order to apply for an absentee or mail-in ballot, you must supply proof of identification."

Furthermore, the later-arriving ballots are not even relevant yet, as none of the mail-in ballots received past the 8 p.m. Nov. 3 cutoff have been included in the counts so far. Counties are keeping those ballots separate so they can be distinguished in case of further litigation.

Michigan

Trump falsely claimed he "won" Michigan, because he was up in the vote count on election night. But of course, the votes were still being counted, and Biden is now ahead by more than 146,000 with 99% of the votes in. All major news organizations, including Fox News, have called the state for Biden.

The president claimed: "Our campaign has been denied access to observe any counting in Detroit." But his own campaign hasn't alleged that. Instead, the campaign has complained about not getting "meaningful access" to observe the counting in "numerous" locations, which it does not identify.

Trump campaign manager Bill Stepien said in a Nov. 4 statement: "President Trump's campaign has not been provided with meaningful access to numerous counting locations to observe the opening of ballots and the counting process, as guaranteed by Michigan law. We have filed suit today in the Michigan Court of Claims to halt counting until meaningful access has been granted."

In a court documents, Jonathan Brater, director of the Michigan Bureau of Elections, said, "I am not aware of any complaints received by the Bureau of Elections that an election inspector was not allowed to be present at an absent voter counting board in any jurisdiction in this State."

The Trump campaign lawsuit, which a state judge dismissed, charged that Michigan's "absent voter counting boards" weren't complying with a statute to have "[a]t all times, at least 1 election inspector from each major political party ... present at the absent voter counting place."

The suit also said election "challengers"—who are not the same as political party inspectors—weren't able to observe video of ballot drop boxes, charging this violated the state Constitution. It named one individual—Eric Ostergren, an election challenger, who claimed he was told to leave the Oakland County counting board. Oakland County is part of the Detroit metropolitan area.

Brater further said that state law exempts drop boxes ordered before October 1 from video surveillance requirements.

Trump appeared to reference a debunked claim from a conservative website when he said the "final batch" of votes in Detroit "did not arrive until 4 in the morning. And even though the polls closed at 8 o'clock, so they brought it in and the batches came in and nobody knew where they came from."

A video posted by a site called Texas Scorecard turned out to show a TV news photographer bringing equipment to the Detroit voting center in the early morning hours of Nov. 4. The video doesn't show any ballots at all. Instead, it shows a man unloading a black box from a white van and putting it into a wagon that he wheels into the TCF Center in Detroit. The website then claims then is "suspicious."

Ross Jones, an investigative reporter for WXYZ-TV, said on Twitter: "The 'ballot thief' was my photographer. He was bringing down equipment for our 12-hour shift."

This "absolute garbage" claim, in Jones' words, was tweeted by the president's son Eric.

Trump distorted an incident at the TCF Center in Detroit in the afternoon of Nov. 4 in which some poll observers, of both parties, and others were barred from entering the counting hall because it was at capacity.

Reuters reported: "Emotions were running high on Wednesday afternoon in downtown Detroit, where city election officials blocked about 30 people, mostly Republicans, from entering the vote-counting hall at TCF Center due to capacity restrictions to fight the spread of COVID-19."

Reuters went on to say "Democrats said they had also been barred," quoting one Democrat poll observer by name.

Trump said that the windows of the counting area were blocked with "large pieces of cardboard," adding: "They didn't want anybody seeing the counting, even though these were observers who were legal observers that were supposed to be there."

Poll officials did block the windows "with pizza boxes and cardboard to prevent challengers from viewing inside," Reuters said. But Trump's implication that no one was observing the vote into the hall is false.

Lawrence Garcia, Detroit's corporation counsel and an election commissioner, said more election challengers couldn't enter the hall because it had hit the permitted capacity for each party, according to Crain's Detroit Business.

Finally, Trump claimed, "Poll workers in Michigan were duplicating ballots." We don't know what Trump is talking about; we asked his campaign but haven't received a response. The president further said: "But when our observers attempted to challenge the activity, those poll workers jumped in front of the volunteers to block their views so that they couldn't see what they were doing and it became a little bit dangerous."

The only reference we could find to duplicating ballots is a comment—in a Detroit News article—by Christopher Schormak, an election challenger with the Election Integrity Fund, a project of the conservative Thomas More Society law firm, who said military and overseas ballots "won't feed into the machine," so they "have to be duplicated and double-checked by another worker."

Schormak didn't allege anything was nefarious or fraudulent about that.

Georgia

Trump made several unfounded, baseless and specious claims about alleged election counting issues in Georgia, where Biden pulled into a slight lead over the president, according to counts as of the morning of Nov. 6.

In a Nov. 6 press conference, the morning after Trump spoke, Georgia Voting System Implementation Manager Gabriel Sterling, a Republican, said state officials have not seen any evidence of widespread voter fraud.

"Are we seeing any widespread fraud? Are we seeing anything that makes us question the outcome of the election?" Sterling said. "We are not seeing any widespread irregularities."

Here are some of Trump's specific claims.

> Trump: Likewise in Georgia, I won by a lot, a lot, with a lead of over getting close to 300,000 votes on election night in Georgia. And by the way, got whittled down and now it's getting to be to a point where I'll go from winning by a lot to perhaps being even down a little bit. In Georgia, a pipe burst in a far away location, totally unrelated to the location of what was happening and they stopped counting for four hours. And a lot of things happened. The election apparatus in Georgia is run by Democrats.

There are several misleading statements here. Trump did not "win" the state by a lot (or at all), though he is correct that he was leading in the vote tallies on election night. But as we have written repeatedly, vote counting always goes past Election Day. There's nothing unusual about that. Like most states, Georgia could not start counting mail-in ballots until the day of the election, and it had roughly 1.3 million mail-in ballots returned and accepted. As has been in the case in other states, most of the mail-in ballots being counted in the days after the election broke in Biden's favor.

As for Trump's claim that "a pipe burst in a far away location, totally unrelated to the location of what was happening and they stopped counting for four hours," there's some truth in that, though there's no evidence that it ultimately affected vote tallies in any way.

As the Atlanta Journal-Constitution reported, a water leak at State Farm Arena in Atlanta, which serves as a ballot processing site, caused a several hours delay in vote-counting on election night. No ballots were damaged, and vote processing resumed normally.

Finally, Trump is wrong to say, "The election apparatus in Georgia is run by Democrats." Georgia has a Republican governor. Georgia's secretary of state, Brad Raffensperger—who oversees elections—is a Republican. And the state's voting implementation manager, Sterling, is a Republican.

Asked at a press conference on Nov. 6 about Trump's comment, Sterling said, "I'm not going to try to get into the president's actual mindset on that, because there are Republicans who are involved, there are Democrats involved at different levels. It's sort of a shared service delivery model. There are Republican election directors. There are Democrat election directors. Obviously, Secretary Raffensperger is a Republican. I'm a Republican. I don't make any bones about that. … In general, we have people who have partisan beliefs, but the job of elections directors and this office is to count every legal vote, follow the law and assure that every legal vote is counted, and the will and intent of the voters is met."

> Trump: The 11th Circuit ruled that in Georgia, the votes have been in by Election Day, that they should be in by Election Day, and they weren't. Votes are coming in after Election Day. And they had a ruling already that you have to have the votes in by

Election Day. To the best of my knowledge, votes should be in by Election Day, and they didn't do that.

It's true that Georgia requires ballots to be received by the close of the polls on Election Day if they are to be counted. (There are 22 states that allow ballots postmarked by Election Day and received in the days after the election to be counted, but Georgia is not one of them.) As Trump noted, the 11th US Circuit Court of Appeals in early October reinstated the Election Day deadline for Georgia voters to return their absentee ballots.

But there is no evidence that any votes received after Election Day are being counted in Georgia, as the president claimed.

The Trump campaign and the Georgia Republican Party filed a lawsuit that included an affidavit from a Republican poll observer who expressed concern that 53 ballots may have been received in Chatham County after the 7 p.m. deadline on Election Day but intermingled with on-time ballots.

Colin McRae, chair of the Chatham County registrars board, testified in a hearing that he reviewed all of the 53 ballots in question and verified that each was time-stamped as having been received before the deadline. Sabrina German, director of the registrars office, told the Atlanta Journal-Constitution that the 53 ballots had initially been separated and flagged for further review, but were received on time. (As of Thursday morning, McRae said, 41 ballots in Chatham County arrived too late, and will not be counted.)

Superior Court Judge James Bass dismissed the Republican lawsuit, stating: "[T]he Court finds that there is no evidence that the ballots referenced in the petition were received after 7:00 p.m. on election day, thereby making those ballots invalid."

> Trump: We've also been denied access to observe in critical places in Georgia.

There's also no evidence of this.

David Shafer, chairman of the Georgia Republican Party, tweeted complaints about at least two instances of alleged obstruction of Republican observers, but there doesn't appear to be much to either of those.

In one case, Shafer complained about workers in a tabulation center in Fulton County "operating a fork lift between the place the ballot scanners are located and the area our observers have been instructed to stand."

In another tweet on the afternoon after Election Day, Shafer alleged, "Fulton County told our observers last night to go home because they were closing up and then continued to count ballots in secret."

But Fulton County officials say that's not true. According to the Associated Press, Rick Barron, the county elections supervisor, told the county board of commissioners "that when he learned staffers were dismissed at 10:30 p.m. Tuesday night, he advised that some of them needed to stay, county spokeswoman Jessica Corbitt said in an email."

"Based on that directive, a smaller crew continued to work through the night," Corbitt told the AP. "It may be possible that observers left at the time the majority of the staff left, but from the information we have, the processing area was never closed to observers."

In a press conference on Nov. 6, Raffensperger, Georgia's Republican secretary of state, said that while there have been allegations in other states about monitors not being allowed to watch the counts, "In Georgia, this process is and will remain open and transparent to monitors."

North Carolina

Trump complained about developments in North Carolina, even though he continues to lead in the Tar Heel State. Trump is ahead by 76,701 votes with 94% of the expected total in.

> Trump: We were ahead in vote in North Carolina by a lot, a tremendous number of votes, and we're still ahead by a lot, but not as many because they're finding ballots all of a sudden. "Oh, we have some mail-in ballots." It's amazing how those mail-in

ballots are so one-sided too. I know that it's supposed to be to the advantage of the Democrats, but in all cases they're so one-sided.

It's no surprise that the mail-in votes are "so one-sided" in favor of the Democrats. Democrats urged their voters to vote via the mail in the midst of the COVID-19 pandemic, while Trump repeatedly assailed mail-in voting. In North Carolina, Democrats requested 669,285 mail ballots—more than twice as many as the 288,393 requested by Republicans, according to the US Elections Project.

And there is no evidence that anyone was "finding ballots all of a sudden."

Trump complained about vote counting in North Carolina early in the morning after Election Day, saying he had a lead and then "all of a sudden everything just stopped." But Patrick Gannon, public information director for the North Carolina State Board of Elections, told us in an email that "North Carolina stopped counting votes on election night because there were no more votes to count at that time."

The state will accept and count absentee ballots that arrive by Nov. 12, as long as they are postmarked by Election Day. It is also assessing and counting provisional ballots. The state is not expected to update its vote totals until next week. North Carolina has not been called by the Associated Press or other news organizations that project the results.

Wisconsin

Trump said, "In Wisconsin, we did likewise fantastically well, and that got whittled down. In every case, they got whittled down."

Trump was seemingly ahead in Wisconsin at the end of the day on Nov. 3, but that was before many of the mail-in ballots were counted. State law prevented election officials from counting absentee ballots before polls opened on Election Day.

As the Milwaukee Journal Sentinel explained: "Biden overtook Trump in the early morning hours when Milwaukee reported its roughly 170,000 absentee votes, which were overwhelmingly Democratic. Then early morning returns from Green Bay and Kenosha on Wednesday added to his slender lead. Trump had nurtured a lead of more than 100,000 votes before those returns came in."

News organizations later declared Biden the projected winner in Wisconsin, with unofficial results showing he received 1,630,568 votes to Trump's 1,610,030.

The Capital Times in Wisconsin had warned its readers ahead of time that it was unlikely a winner would be declared on election night.

"Because so many are voting by absentee ballot this fall, election workers will face longer-than-normal processing times as they move to accurately count votes throughout the day Tuesday—work that, by state law, can't start until 7 a.m., when polls open," the Capital Times said. "While there was some bipartisan support for changing that law or making other adjustments, nothing was enacted, making it unlikely that unofficial statewide results will be known here Tuesday."

Arizona

Trump notably has not called for votes to stop being counted in Arizona, where he currently trails Biden.

"Today, we're on track to win Arizona," the president said in his remarks. "We only need to carry, I guess, 55% of the remaining vote, 55% margins, and that's a margin that we've significantly exceeded. So we'll see what happens with that, but we're on track to do okay in Arizona."

In contrast to states where Trump lost his lead as absentee and mail-in ballots were counted, those ballots are helping him shrink Biden's lead in Arizona.

As the Arizona Republic reported:

> Arizona Republic, Nov. 5: President Donald Trump inched closer to former Vice President Joe Biden as results from Thursday's ballot counting were released, but he fell off the pace needed to win Arizona's 11 electoral votes.

Trump won 55.6% of the ballots counted in Maricopa County on Thursday to Biden's 41.7%. It was a great showing, but Trump's challenge is he needs more than 57% of the outstanding votes to win.

Statewide, Trump chipped away 22,000 votes from Biden's lead, closing the gap to 46,667 votes as of 9:30 p.m. Thursday. But unless the next batches of votes show Trump with a higher percentage than what the president managed Thursday, he will fall short.

The Arizona Republic said there were 300,000 votes left to count as of Thursday evening.

Fox News called Arizona for Biden late on election night, and the Associated Press made the call for Biden early in the morning the following day. Other news organizations have not projected a winner.

Trump Loyalists Would Not See That Joe Biden's Victory Was Indisputable

Lily Hay Newman

Lily Hay Newman is a senior writer at Wired, *focused on information security, digital privacy, and hacking. She previously worked as a technology reporter at* Slate *and was the staff writer for Future Tense, a publication and project of Slate, the New America Foundation, and Arizona State University. Additionally her work has appeared in Gizmodo, Fast Company, IEEE Spectrum, and Popular Mechanics. She lives in New York City.*

A bitter campaign season marked by extreme ideological disputes and an unprecedented pandemic is now over. On Saturday morning, the Associated Press and other media outlets declared Joe Biden the winner of the 2020 United States presidential election after four days of electoral uncertainty. And despite Donald Trump's repeated insistence to the contrary, there has been no sign whatsoever of intentional voter fraud.

As he had telegraphed for months before Election Day, incumbent Donald Trump has attempted to discredit this year's electoral process on the grounds that expanded mail voting and the counting delays it caused in some states represent large-scale fraud. "If you count the legal votes, I easily win the election!" Trump said in an all-caps campaign statement on Thursday. "If you count the illegal and late votes, they can steal the election from us!" In a press conference Thursday evening, Trump unleashed a torrent of lies centered on discrediting the electoral system in states he seemed poised to lose.

Despite those claims, Trump and his campaign have presented no actual evidence of "illegal" votes at all. And the ballots Trump describes as "late" were all cast on or before

"Joe Biden Won—and Not Because of Voter Fraud," by Lily Hay Newman, *Wired*, November 7, 2020. Reprinted by permission.

Election Day. In fact, in spite of the daunting challenges posed by the pandemic, Election Day and the early and absentee voting leading up to it went as smoothly as it could have. Consider what has already been accomplished: Roughly 160 million people voted, a record turnout representing about two-thirds of all eligible voters.

Trump has not yet conceded the race, and seems unlikely to anytime soon. There will likely be a recount in Georgia, because the victory margin is so close, and there could be others in states like Wisconsin as well. But as numerous courts have already signaled in response to a volley of spurious lawsuits filed by Trump's campaign, every aspect of the election was fully legitimate. If it weren't, you'd know it by now.

The Mail Voting Is All Right

One of the Trump campaign's core gripes is that expanded absentee by-mail voting, motivated by the pandemic, was actually a plot by Democrats to increase the party's voter turnout and enable fraud.

"Democrat officials never believed they could win this election honestly," Trump said in his Thursday evening press conference. "That's why they did the mail-in ballots, where there's tremendous corruption and fraud going on."

For one thing, research indicates that expanding mail voting doesn't necessarily benefit Democrats in every instance anyway. (In this case, Trump explicitly telling his supporters not to vote by mail may have led to more partisan imbalance than usual.) But even more important, local and state election officials around the country deployed expanded mail voting as a nonpartisan way to reduce crowding at polling places and make it easier for people to have a contactless voting experience.

To Republican leadership, though, an unprecedented pandemic that has killed more than 200,000 people in the US alone has not been a convincing reason to deploy systemic safety measures.

"They used Covid as an excuse, and it was allowed to happen, and it is just wrong, and it is rigged," GOP chair Ronna McDaniel told FOX News on Thursday.

The Trump campaign particularly took issue with states like Nevada and California that for the first time sent mail ballots to all registered voters this year because of the pandemic. At the end of September a Nevada judge dismissed a Trump lawsuit aiming to block the practice in the state. Ahead of Election Day on Monday, a judge in Carson City, Nevada, also dismissed a suit by the Trump reelection campaign aimed at changing how Democratic-leaning Clark County verifies signatures and counts mail ballots.

On Thursday, the Trump campaign planned to file a lawsuit that would challenge 10,000 Nevada mail ballots. The campaign alleges that the ballots were submitted by voters who no longer live in the state or are dead. Trump is pursuing similar suits in other states as well, so far without much success.

Regardless, with more than 150 million votes counted, there's no evidence of mail vote-related fraud and certainly not on a scale that would change the results of the election. Besides, even Trump himself may not be as suspicious of mail voting as he seems. "Early voting and vote-by-mail start TODAY in ARIZONA!" he tweeted at the beginning of October. "We want all eligible voters to vote, and have it counted! Request your vote-by-mail ballot by clicking below!"

Only Election Day (or Earlier) Votes Have Been Counted

In his Thursday evening press conference, President Trump laid out two of his core concerns. "They're finding ballots all of a sudden," he said of the Democrats. "Votes are coming in after Election Day. And they had a ruling already [in Georgia] that you have to have the votes in by Election Day … In Pennsylvania, partisan Democrats have allowed ballots in the state to be received three days after the election."

Counting, auditing, and canvassing always takes time after an election, and each state determines its deadlines for when mail ballots must be postmarked and received. Pennsylvania originally set Election Day as the deadline to receive absentee by-mail ballots but didn't list a postmark deadline. In October, the state revised the timeline so ballots postmarked through Election Day would be counted if they were received by 5 pm Friday (today) local time. A federal court and the Supreme Court both upheld the change. In Georgia, absentee ballots sent from overseas must be postmarked by Election Day but will be accepted through today.

Regardless of the specifics in each state, multiple days of processing does not mean that late absentee ballots are being counted or that states are changing their deadlines on the fly. Pennsylvania in particular was expected to count late into the week, because of a state law that prevented officials from starting to count mail ballots in advance of Election Day.

"There has never been, in modern history, a federal election in the United States where we had official results on Election Day," says Larry Norden, deputy director of the Brennan Center's Democracy Program at New York University School of Law. "It is quite normal for counting to take more than one day. Official tallies in federal elections almost always take several days to weeks, and the reason is simple: We want to make sure the count is accurate."

Observers Have Had Access All Along

For those concerned about the legality of various mail ballot receipt deadlines and vote tallying after Election Day, the counting and canvassing processes are open to campaign observers and, in most states, the public. In Michigan and especially Pennsylvania, the Trump campaign alleges that ballot processing is being done in secret.

"We are suing to stop Democrat election officials from hiding the ballot counting and processing from our Republican poll observers," deputy campaign manager Justin Clark said in a statement on Wednesday. Philadelphia's public livestream of the process was apparently not an adequate gesture. On Thursday evening, a district judge dismissed the Trump campaign's filing earlier that afternoon to halt counting in Philadelphia over lack of Republican observers. In a hearing, campaign officials admitted—contrary to Trump's public claims—that they in fact had been allowed to send observers into vote-processing facilities. The issue they raised was not being allowed to send as many as the Democrats had. Judge Paul Diamond, who became increasingly exasperated throughout the hearing, suggested brokering a set maximum number of observers for each party. The group eventually landed on 60 each.

"By having the public observation, that holds people accountable—making sure that people can see what you're doing, why you're doing it, and that you're following the rules," Marian Schneider, an election and voting rights consultant for the ACLU of Pennsylvania and the former president of the election integrity nonprofit Verified Voting told WIRED in August. "It's just part of our democracy to have processes in place that allow citizens to participate as observers."

And while the Trump campaign paints the situation as dishonest Democrats gallivanting about in party strongholds, there's representation from both parties among election officials if you look across all of the districts and states that needed more time to declare preliminary results. Nevada has a Republican secretary of state, and Georgia has both a Republican governor and secretary of state.

Election Officials Are Already Monitoring for Fraud

Voting fraud can happen, and over the past year President Trump has frantically highlighted isolated examples around the country of investigations that exposed issues. But research—including

Were the Capitol Rioters Truly Protesting the Results of the Presidential Election?

findings from right-leaning policy groups—has consistently shown that voting fraud is very rare and almost never shows up on a scale that would substantially impact a major election. The fact that Trump has been able to find examples at all, though, speaks instead to the monitoring measures that election officials have in place to catch wrongful votes.

Exact strategies vary by state, but all monitor for double voting, vet absentee ballots for correct personal data like Social Security number and signature matches, and number or otherwise track ballots to ensure that random forgeries can't just make their way into the pile. Any ballot that has an inconsistency, looks suspicious, or is a provisional ballot gets pulled for manual review.

"When it comes to vote-by-mail and voter impersonation, you might get away with impersonating a small number of voters, but you won't swing the election, and if you do anything at scale you're going to get found out," says Ben Adida, executive director of VotingWorks, a nonprofit developer of open source voting machines and election auditing software. "I don't worry about the risk of fraud, because there are processes in place for ensuring everybody only gets to vote once."

The decentralized, state-controlled nature of US elections gives the system even more resilience. In spite of the Trump campaign's general impatience, unsupported allegations, and incendiary rhetoric, there is no one centralized body the campaign can lobby to push results out before they're ready. They can't universally undermine the quality controls that make the process time consuming. And while it's always possible (though, again, extremely unlikely) that a bad actor manipulated ballots during voting, it would require a massive inside job—while the country, the world, and Trump campaign observers are watching—to execute a massive, intentional fraud campaign during counting.

Trump Is Lighting a Powder Keg

Despite the lack of evidence to support the Trump campaign's allegations, the president's statements and those of other GOP leaders have stoked anxiety and unrest. Trump supporters in both Detroit and Phoenix protested outside ballot-processing sites on Wednesday, alternately calling for officials to "count the votes" and "stop the count." In Maricopa County, Arizona, officials shut down the election office just after 9 pm local time, over fears that the protest could become violent.

Meanwhile, social networks have been grappling with how to handle false information about vote processing. On Thursday, Facebook removed a group with more than 360,000 members called "STOP THE STEAL" for violating its policies. Twitter added misinformation warnings to a number of Trump's tweets throughout the week, and flagged other posts as well, including one from Donald Trump Jr. that said, "The best thing for America's future is for @realDonaldTrump to go to total war over this election." YouTube and Twitter both suspended former White House adviser Steve Bannon's web show and removed an episode in which Bannon literally called for the beheading of top US pandemic expert Anthony Fauci and FBI director Christopher Wray.

The most important thing to remember, though, is that despite fanning those flames, the Trump campaign and its supporters have yet to produce any actual evidence of wrongdoing. It has lost multiple court cases already in its opening bid to toss wrenches into democracy's gears. And the Organization for Security and Co-operation in Europe, which sent independent observers to monitor US Election Day at the request of the federal government, called claims of election fraud "evidence-deficient" in its preliminary report on Wednesday night.

"The 3 November general elections were competitive and well managed despite legal uncertainties and logistical challenges," the OSCE wrote. It did, though, find one potential threat to the integrity of the vote: "Baseless allegations of systematic deficiencies, notably by the incumbent president, including on election night, harm public trust in democratic institutions."

Expect those baseless allegations to continue with increasing volume. But ultimately, it's not Donald Trump who gets to decide the next president of the United States. It's the voters. And they've chosen Joe Biden.

Claims of Voter Fraud Have a Long History in America
David Litt

David Litt is an American political speechwriter and author of the comedic memoir Thanks, Obama: My Hopey Changey White House Years.

Texas's lieutenant governor, Dan Patrick, was supposed to be a whole lot poorer by now.

On 11 November, eight days after the presidential election and four days after the networks called the race for Joe Biden, the conservative talk radio host turned Republican politician launched a bounty hunt. Any tipsters who could provide evidence of voter fraud that led to a criminal conviction would receive at least $25,000, up to a grand total of $1m. The money was set to come from Patrick's campaign, not his personal account. Still, the point remains: if voter fraud was rampant, as President Trump and leading Republicans have repeatedly claimed, Patrick's million-dollar fund should have run dry long ago.

As it stands, Patrick's campaign finances are in far better shape than his credibility. To date, it appears he has paid out a grand total of zero dollars and zero cents.

Patrick stands out for his willingness to put his donors' money where his mouth was. But his million-dollar effort was just a small part of the largest voter-fraud hunt in American history. Never in American history have self-proclaimed fraud-fighters been given more attention, resources and time to prove their case—that a major election was stolen through what they've dubbed "illegal votes."

Instead, they've done the opposite. The 2020 election, and Trump's attempt to overturn it, will leave us with plenty of reasons

"Claims of 'Voter Fraud' Have a Long History in America. And They Are False," by David Litt, *Guardian*, December 4, 2020. Reprinted by permission.

to remain concerned about the health of our democracy. But the idea that our political process has been compromised by widespread fraud isn't among them. It's time to retire the voter-fraud myth for good.

Falsely claiming voter fraud is a tradition nearly as old as American democracy itself. Take, for example, early 19th-century New Jersey. Under the state's original constitution, some women had the right to vote, and some politicians (namely those of the Federalist party) felt they would be more likely to win elections if those rights were taken away. But stripping eligible voters of their rights for purely partisan reasons was unseemly, even by 1800s standards, so ambitious lawmakers came up with an excuse. Men, they charged, were casting their ballots, slipping into petticoats, and then voting a second time. The only way to prevent this gender-bending fraud was to eliminate women's voting rights entirely.

As a logical argument, the anti-fraud case for disenfranchising women made little sense. But logic was never the point. In 1807, aided by their theoretically principled excuse for their blatantly partisan power grab, the New Jersey legislature ended their state's experiment in women's suffrage.

As more Americans won voting rights on paper, and the two-party system became more entrenched in our political process, voter fraud remained a convenient excuse for disenfranchising eligible voters. In the 1830s, on the theory that cities couldn't be trusted to hold honest elections, Pennsylvania passed a voter registration law that applied to the city of Philadelphia and nowhere else. "Although the proclaimed goal of the law was to reduce fraud," writes Alexander Keyssar in The Right to Vote, "opponents insisted that its real intent was to reduce the participation of the poor, who were frequently not home when assessors came by."

Not surprisingly, false claims of fraud also played an important role in propping up segregation. In 1959, Washington parish, Louisiana, "purged" its voter rolls. Local officials claimed they were merely remove illegally registered names from the rolls. In fact, they purged 85% of the parish's African American voters.

This proved too audacious even for the Jim Crow era, and a federal court overturned the parish's purge. But in most cases, courts have given lawmakers the benefit of the doubt. So long as they can plausibly claim to be fighting fraud—or more accurately, so long as they can't be proven not to be fighting fraud—legislators can pass bills restricting access to the ballot, even for eligible voters, and even if the voters affected are clearly more likely to belong to one party than the other.

In other words, when conservative pundit Dick Morris claimed that over a million people voted twice in the 2012 elections, when President Trump alleged that millions of undocumented immigrants cast ballots in 2016, or when Rudy Giuliani dropped his sweaty dud of a bombshell at Four Seasons Total Landscaping, they were taking part in a timeless American tradition. From a moral standpoint, falsely claiming fraud is despicable. But from a political standpoint, it's historically been a win-win: in a best-case scenario you disenfranchise voters in an election that already occurred, and in a worse-case scenario you lay the groundwork for disenfranchising them next time.

Already, Republican politicians are once again using the fear of voter fraud—a fear that exists, to the extent it does, entirely because of baseless claims they generated—as a pretext to attack the voting rights of eligible American citizens. The Texas congressman Dan Crenshaw recently argued that the only way to restore confidence in our elections is to make voter registration far more difficult and outlaw mail-in voting for many if not most Americans. The Florida senator Rick Scott has gone even further. His "fraud-fighting" bill would throw out ballots if a county can't tally them within 24 hours, even if those ballots are legally cast.

It's hardly surprising that politicians like Crenshaw and Scott believe they can get away with turning false claims of voter fraud into the very real disenfranchisement of eligible voters. It's happened many times before. But this time ought to be different. Egged on by the would-be authoritarian in the White House, election results have been challenged in at least six states. Dozens of lawsuits have been filed in an attempt to delay or overturn the certification of the final tallies. Hearings have been held. The attorney general, Bill Barr, in a frightening break with established Department of Justice procedure, authorized federal prosecutors to investigate credible fraud claims even if doing so would appear political.

The results? The Trump administration is now a 39-time loser in court. A parade of frustrated judges, many appointed by Trump himself, have written blistering opinions pointing out that the president and his allies have no basis for their claims. Even Trump's own lawyers have admitted under questioning that they're not alleging fraud because they have no evidence with which to do so. Inside the conservative echo chamber, the Republican party's attacks on the integrity of our elections will sow doubt and distrust in our political process. But in the real world, the idea that marquee elections are being stolen via voter fraud has now been disproven beyond a reasonable doubt.

Which means that, barring real evidence to the contrary, it's time for our institutions to stop taking partisan claims of voter fraud seriously. Reporters should treat allegations of a fraudulent election the way they treat birtherism or QAnon—as pure conspiracy theory. Courts should stop giving self-proclaimed fraud-fighters the benefit of the doubt, and instead demand that they substantiate their allegations before barring eligible Americans from the ballot box. The handful of Republican politicians who, to their lasting credit, condemned Trump's attempts to manipulate the most recent election should be equally forceful about attempts to manipulate future ones.

This year, false claims of fraud weren't enough to overturn an election. But next time we may not be so lucky. Trump is not the first American to embrace the voter-fraud myth for his political advantage, but if American democracy is to survive, he ought to be the last.

January 6 Brought Trump to a True Level of Fascism

Paul Nicholas Jackson

Paul Nicholas Jackson is associate professor and senior lecturer in history at the University of Northampton, where he specializes in fascism and the extreme right. He is editor of Bloomsbury's book series A Modern History of Politics and Violence.

Since coming to prominence, Donald Trump's politics has regularly been likened to fascism. Many experts within fascism studies have tried to engage with wider media and political debates on the relevance (or otherwise) of such comparisons. Most have urged that contrasts should be drawn between the fascist past and whatever we might want to term the present, though no-one seems to suggest there are no similarities between Trump's politics and fascism (however it may be defined). Moreover, many have suggested that fascist elements operate within at least part of the wider movement—or set of movements—that have developed around Trump's politics.

Following the unprecedented events of 6 January 2021 in America, some voices in this debate also felt that things had changed. Most notably, Robert Paxton, who had previously resisted categorising Trump as a fascist, wrote an article for Newsweek explaining: "Trump's incitement of the invasion of the Capitol on January 6, 2020 removes my objection to the fascist label. His open encouragement of civic violence to overturn an election crosses a red line. The label now seems not just acceptable but necessary."[1]

At *Fascism*, we have invited leading academics with connections to the journal and those who are familiar with

---

"Debate: Donald Trump and Fascism Studies," by Paul Nicholas Jackson, *Fascism*, June 24, 2021, https://doi.org/10.1163/22116257-10010009. Licensed under CC BY 4.0 International.

debates within fascism studies, to offer thoughts on how to consider the complex relationship between fascism, the politics of Donald Trump, and the wider maga movement. We asked contributors to limit their comments to a short statement of around five hundred words, and these collectively have been able to capture a range of important observations for future scholarly analysis of these issues. It is hoped these commentaries will help develop this debate in analytically constructive ways, and in particular prove useful for those engaged in researching contemporary forms of fascism, as well as the wider extreme and populist radical right.

Mattias Gardell, Professor at the Centre for Multidisciplinary Studies on Racism, University of Uppsala

Does Trump and the political force he unleashed signal the return of fascism to mainstream politics? If so, in what respect? Discussing whether Trump himself is a fascist may not be the most fruitful endeavour. Trump may be many things; a narcissist with a grandiose sense of self, a compulsive confabulator, a populist charlatan, but there is not much to indicate that he is politically conscious, or even interested enough to have adopted an ideology of any sort, including fascism. Yet, his maga campaign positioned the key fascist vision of national rebirth at the centre of political attention, and we are well advised to remember that also Hitler and Mussolini could be dismissed as egomaniacs, half-insane rascals, big-mouths, and buffoons, by mainstream commentators at the time.

The maga vision obviously touches a nerve in popular, predominantly white, American imagination, nurtured by layers of (not always frictionless) banal nationalism, Americanism, nativism, white supremacy, manifest destiny, and racialized discourse and practice. White liberal Americans were chocked when Trump in 2016 gained 63 million votes, Black Americans less so. "This is the US we know," one of my old African American interlocutors said.

If fascism gains a hold in the mainstream, it will grow from within. This informs us that fascism should not be seen as alien to, but part of, the societies in which it competes for hegemony. Of course, no society exists in isolation. The breakthrough of Trump and the maga campaign cannot only be explained by domestic factors, but should also be studied in relation to the current surge of radical nationalisms around the world, and the process of globalization they are part and protest of.

A key driver of the maga campaign is politicized nostalgia, by which the anxieties of the present are contrasted to the imagined happiness of a lost/stolen/abandoned, but not undead past. Of course, nostalgia is not exclusive to fascism, but permeates popular culture as evidenced by retro style trends in design, fashion, art, music, and film. This is important as a return of fascist elements to mainstream politics requires their embeddedness in popular desire. Marketing the past may make people miss what they never had, and hence cannot have lost, which may open an avenue for mainstreaming the yearning to "Make the Nation Great Again."

The maga vision is vague enough to allow people from various walks of life to project different hopes of what it may entail. Most Trump voters were not necessarily fascist, but some were. Galvanized by the maga call was a heterogenous milieu of white nationalists, radical traditionalists, alt-right identitarians, conspiracy exposers, militias, neo-confederates, and sovereign citizens that Trump knowingly catered to. Millions of Americans shared the dream of national rebirth, though not necessarily what it was supposed to mean. By 2020, some were disenchanted with what they had got. However, most remained enthused, and willing to dismiss every contradiction in Trump's words and deeds, and Trump increased his support by 11 million votes. Politics does not only depend on rational reason, but has an important affective dimension which fascism frequently caters to.

Trump's ousting will hardly be the end of story. Even if he sticks to golf and his Florida resort, Trump's 74 million voters and their grievances are still out there, and there are already contenders to his throne elected to congress and other institutions of mainstream politics.

Ruth Wodak, Emerita Distinguished Professor of Discourse Studies at Lancaster University

Many papers are currently discussing the so-called "Trump-phenomenon": Is Trump himself a fascist? Is Trumpism a fascist movement? Is it still possible to use the concept of "fascism" or does the term only refer to Mussolini's Fascism, Austro-Fascism, Mosley's Blackshirts or Spanish Franquismo of the 1920s and 1930s? How do concepts such as "alt-right," "ultra-nationalism," "extreme-right," "illiberalism," "neo-authoritarianism," "identitarianism" (and many more) relate to "fascism" per se? Are these sanitizing, euphemistic concepts, attempting to avoid the negative connotations of the original term?

Actually, it does not make sense to lose oneself in terminological debates. Nor is it useful to speculate if Trump is or is not a fascist. Scholars have not had the chance to observe Trump's "backstage" to be able to judge his personality features, apart from his publicly staged performances. Clearly however, when studying his biography, he frequently changed positions, for example, from supporting the Democrats to standing as Republican presidential candidate. In his thirst for power, money and public recognition, Trump could be viewed as an "entertaining, very persuasive salesman," selling whatever it takes to achieve his aims, supported (and instrumentalized) by his ideologues.

Accordingly, following semioticians and discourse analysts such as Umberto Eco, Michael Billig and John E Richardson, a focus on the range of discursive and material practices realizing and implementing the ideological positions of the Trump administration, fostered by ideologues such as Steven Bannon, is recommended. Moreover, the socio-political, historical as well as situative contexts are relevant: Trump(ism) did not occur spontaneously; its ideological roots and rhetoric reach back to other nativist, extremist politicians like Barry Goldwater and fundamentalist, conservative movements like the Tea-Party which defied Barack Obama's presidency, supported and financed by (huge parts of) the gop, media tycoons, and corporatism. Such movements which strategically manipulate the frustrations and anxieties of many people, while distracting them from their objective source, through offering emotionally and ideologically laden concepts such as obedience, honour, duty, the fatherland or race, and focusing on "enemies" (i.e., scapegoats) who allegedly threaten the longed-for sense of community, can be defined as fascist.[2]

Trump's rhetoric applies salient discursive practices of fascism, both on-line and offline. On the one hand, he was the figurehead via his rallies and propagandistic Twitter politics (34,000 Tweets in the period of June 2015 until 8 January 2021); simultaneously, many diverse groupuscules on manifold digital platforms assembled under (t)his umbrella, all connected with each other to construct a "digital fascism."[3] Scandalisation, provocation, transgression of taboos, hate incitement, and violation of norms and conventions were part and parcel of Trump's daily performance. Of course, such incidents not only guarantee many headlines and much (positive and negative) resonance; they also serve as distraction (i.e. "dead cat-strategy") from specific policies intended to challenge and undermine democratic institutions, such as independent legislation, press freedom or democratic elections.

Typically, the rhetoric of Trump and his followers was based on the Manichean division of "us" (the "real, pure, white" Americans) and "them" (Muslims, migrants, refugees, leftists and liberals, intellectuals, etc.); on mobilizing weaponized chants at rallies; and on encouraging his supporters to use violence against alleged enemies. As historian Timothy Snyder rightly maintained, "this [Trumpism] has everything to do with race from top to bottom."[4] Trump explicitly contemplated that

Hillary Clinton should be assassinated while continuously repeating the phrase "crooked Hillary"; and he launched traditional antisemitic tropes of a "Jewish World Conspiracy" claiming that philanthropist George Soros was responsible both for the influx of so-called "illegal migrants" from Mexico and for political opposition. Moreover, serious media and facts were delegitimized, "alternative facts" and lies legitimized. He openly sided with "Proud Boys" and equated antisemitic, white supremacists with anti-fascist demonstrators. Such "dangerous speech"[5] was further enhanced by expressions of blatant machismo and misogyny. Obviously, discursive practices constitute and manifest realities—Trump's rhetoric thus accompanied and also enabled authoritarian policies and practices.

Benjamin R. Teitelbaum, Assistant Professor of Ethnomusicology and International Affairs, University of Colorado Boulder

Is fascism a historic or a diachronic phenomenon? If it is the latter, do today's far-right populists qualify as fascists?

I've always felt uninspired by these discussions because I consider their conditions too trivial. We can identify similarities and dissimilarities among far-rightists past and present, and we can argue that some generic visions and behaviours are more distinguishing of historic fascism, at least, than others. But I don't see how those analyses could allow us to take the crucial final step: to allege that a contemporary actor is not merely fascist-like but fully fascist. And yet as I equivocate in that historiographical debate, I unequivocally reject using the term to refer to figures like Donald Trump today, and do so based on epistemological and pedagogical grounds.

Invoking the term today signals an end of inquiry. Whereas ideological mappings of the contemporary far-right might include jarringly unfamiliar monikers like anarcho-capitalists, race materialists, right-wing nihilists, and so on, everyone thinks they know fascism.

Moreover, if there's one thing everyone knows about fascism, it's that they already know enough. It is the cause that liberal democracies cannot tolerate and the foremost manifestation of humanity's capacity for evil—what's left to say? It follows that professional and lay scholars often reflexively consider fascism as the utmost extreme in radical right-wing politics. If more contemporary far-right movements are regarded as facades concealing something more sinister, that something is fascism. Refer to a cause by another name, and you are participating in the act of deception.

I see little room in these conversations for the public to learn something new—about the past or the present. And it is not just lay audiences who suffer, for fascism talk gives us a dose of something we do not need. Far-right studies suffers from a troubling tendency to relish certainty over curiosity and regularity over inconsistency. It is lop-sided where many other fields strive toward balance, directing its attention heavily in favour of the macro over the micro, the general over the particular, and preferring to emphasize sameness rather than difference when comparing actors across sociocultural context and history. These are prerequisites to issuing condemnations of our subject that are not only impassioned, but simplistic. Multiple incentives drive this ur-paradigm, the most noble is the anxiety of understatement when dealing with political forces that can cause exceptional human suffering; as for physicians, the consequences of overdiagnosis may appear miniscule compared with the opposite. But we are also lured by vanity and the promise that media will amplify our words and names if we escalate the charges against contemporary right-wing radicals.

I would think differently about "fascism" were its contemporary usage something other than a lynchpin of this paradigm; instead it is the banner of our certitudes and the content in our proclamations of our subject's regularity and dulness. I would think differently, also, were our field's challenges of another kind, were they actually (as some critics allege) to be found in excess relativism and apologetics. Until that becomes the case I will seek out labels that do not attempt to explain so much and that deprive us the comfort of familiarity.

David Renton, independent scholar and author of *Fascism: History and Theory* (Pluto Press, 2020)

My sense is that most specialists did not believe that Trump was a fascist prior to 6 January 2021. His occupation of the White House had not significantly increased the authoritarian resources of the US state, he did not build a one-party regime. What is more interesting to ask is therefore whether the coup of 6 January, had it been properly planned, would have taken him "over the edge," to speak, converting a form of aggressive conservatism into something else?

One answer might be to recall that even the figures we know best, Hitler, Mussolini, Mosley, etc, were not born fascists but had to make themselves into the figures they became. We can imagine Trump poised between different political strategies, facing his own insurgent right-wing people, and telling himself: This is the crowd which might yet save my Presidency. In those circumstances, the decision to take power through a coup rather than an election, would have been the recognisable act of a military dictator and potentially that of a fascist. Undoubtedly, it would have changed Trump. He would have given a pledge to his supporters and would have a debt to them afterwards. He would be the same person, with the same previous history, but the logic of his decision to take power outside an election would have changed him.

The problem with the above thoughts, of course, is that they are counterfactuals. Plenty of others have been here before, imagining what almost happened but never did (Niall Ferguson's *Virtual History*[6] is a good example of the flaws of this genre). The coup failed; every impression is that it was not meant to "succeed." It was a protest which found itself far closer to the symbols of power than its participants ever believed. The election was not close; the state never split.

There are two conclusions we could draw from this. Both address the susceptibility of our moment in history to capture by a violent, far-right. In one approach, the centre is surprisingly robust. It turns out that no plausible case could be made in favour of an American dictatorship. Even Trump-appointed judges and lawmakers would not consent to it.

In the other approach, we have just been given a warning, and not from history. Had the voting in the 2020 election been closer, so that a decent argument could have been made that the results were genuinely unclear, Trump would have faced a much more serious opportunity to keep himself in power. If so, we can assume that even more elected Republicans would have supported him, and even the armed forces might possibly have been split. At that point, the comparison with fascism would indeed have become meaningful.

We were supposed to be living in a post-fascist moment. It turns out that our society is more polarised, and more vulnerable to authoritarianism than we like to believe.

Nigel Copsey, Professor of Modern History, Teesside University

As the December 2020 special issue of Fascism bears out, the histories of fascism and anti-fascism are ineluctably interwoven. Nonetheless, there is still a regrettable tendency amongst scholars of fascism, working with their own strict, and rarefied definitions, to demean anti-fascist activism for oversimplification, distortion, and misrepresentation.

So how did self-proclaimed anti-fascists in the US respond to events at Capitol Hill on 6 January 2021? There were those who, not unexpectedly, rushed to label it a "fascist coup." The campaign group, Refuse Fascism, is one example. This group has, since its founding in the wake of Trump's 2016 election, consistently applied the term "fascism" to the Trump/Pence administration. However, there are other self-proclaimed anti-fascists, many aligned to Antifa (which should be differentiated from Refuse Fascism), who are capable of offering a far more nuanced and sophisticated reading.

For It's Going Down (igd), which is the leading digital platform for anarchist, anti-fascist, autonomous anti-capitalist and anti-colonial movements in the US, the crowd at Capitol Hill represented a coalition of "Trumpian forces" and "fascists" and were more precisely disaggregated into "Proud Boys, neo-Nazis, groypers, maga supporters, QAnon followers, covid-truthers, and militia members."[7] This was less an insurrection or revolt than a "permitted fascist temper tantrum."[8]

As a historian drawn to researching anti-fascism (as well as fascism), I am very mindful that anti-fascists often subject their adversaries to misrepresentation. Yet anti-fascists can also be the subject of misrepresentation too, and in some cases, egregiously so. As we have seen, over the course of the last few years the Trump administration, and the Trump-supporting right-wing eco-system, have been instrumental in spreading disinformation about Antifa.

As late as 5 January 2021, Trump was still hankering for Antifa to be classified a "terrorist organisation." On that day—the day before the now infamous "Save America" rally—Trump issued a presidential memorandum directing the Secretary of State to assess whether to classify Antifa a terrorist organisation under 8 usc §1182(a)(3)(B)(vi), and to consider listing Antifa in 9 fam 302.5–4(B)(2)(U), thereby denying entry to the United States of "aliens who have engaged or who are likely to engage in terrorist activity." In one of his final presidential tweets, Trump warned:

> Antifa is a Terrorist Organization, stay out of Washington. Law enforcement is watching you very closely!
> —Donald J. Trump (@realdonaldtrump) january 5, 2021.[9]

Whether or not the timing of this memorandum was deliberate—a way to excuse potential violence by his supporters against counter-protestors on 6 January—is a moot point. Yet Antifa did not show. In their absence, rumours would later abound that Antifa had been amongst the Capitol rioters (a belief that forty per cent of respondents in one recent Anti-Defamation League poll thought true).

Needless to say, the "false-flag" rumours were groundless (like many of the other spurious claims about Antifa that had preceded them). The reality, having recently interviewed anti-fascists activists in the US, is that anti-fascists do exercise significant levels of restraint, both offline and online.[10] Exercising restraint appears more challenging for right-wing extremists, who, according to the adl's Center on Extremism, were responsible for 90 per cent of all extremism-related murders in the United States in 2019. It is not for nothing that Antifa activists will tell you that fascism is an inherently violent ideology.

Raul Cârstocea, Honorary Fellow in European History, University of Leicester

Discussions of "fascism" in our own time need to consider the fact that victory over fascism acted as the foundational myth of the post-war era on both sides of the Cold War, and certainly in the United States of America. Once established as a topos of ultimate evil and in that key decisively linked to Nazi Germany rather than any other regime or movement, "fascism" has become at once an extreme form of politics unlikely to be replicated in its exact historical manifestation, a label most of the contemporary far right except the very fringe will go to lengths to avoid, and a term of abuse for any unsavoury characters or organisations. Assessments of Trump as a "fascist" have to navigate this unstable field, and the term of comparison for most academic and journalistic accounts has indeed been Nazi Germany (or, slightly more capaciously, Hitler and Mussolini).

Yet fascism as a political ideology covered a wide spectrum of individual actors and organisations, lacked an internationally unitary doctrine, and, due to its ultra-nationalism and insistence on its home-grown character, was always more context-specific than either socialism or liberalism. Its character also changed over time, was dependent on the position of the actors and their respective goals, which varied based on whether they were marginal organisations facing state opposition, large-scale movements with a serious bid to political power, or established regimes. Finally, while native fascisms differed greatly from Romania through Belgium to Britain, there were also "para-fascists" and authoritarian regimes that adopted fascist ideological or stylistic trappings without embracing fascism's revolutionary impetus. It is against this background that I believe we need to conceptualise Trump's "fascism" rather than against a simplistic "Hitler" strawman, factoring in also the specifically American roots of his politics, whether they be racism or anti-communism. Results may vary, as they say, and we can conclude with confidence that, whether or not a "fascist" himself, which is becoming less relevant, Trump did radicalise the Republican Party considerably and he did mobilise actual fascists to seek a violent overthrow of the establishment.

A final consideration is that fascism, like most other-isms, means different things to specialists and laymen. It is certainly overused to condemn those who challenge liberal democracy, just as it is used as a misnomer for authoritarianism, racism, antisemitism, or political violence. Here the role of the specialist is certainly one of providing more precision and clarity based on in-depth knowledge of historical fascism, some fundamental tenets discernible beneath the fluidity of its numerous iterations. But it may also be not to be entirely dismissive of the "lay" meanings and to try to understand instead the mechanisms that account for its staying power. This might bring us back to that foundational myth and prompt us to question whether its reassuring narrative is not a blind spot to mutated viral strains that may constitute the 2.0 version of analogue fascism for our digital post-fascist present.

Maria Bucur, Professor, History and Gender Studies, Indiana University Bloomington

The toxic charisma of Donald Trump swept through many spots of the world and took its toll on people in Eastern Europe along the way. In Romania, Trump was popular throughout his presidency with some small exceptions. He was simply America, and that meant not a communist and, in his case, definitely not a leftist. That made him more palatable from the perspective of a population that had come to hate communism with passion, and included a small but constant fringe of fascists posing for decades as anti-communist resisters. Ioan Antonescu's reputation is still pristine among a small group of enthusiasts, and Ioan Gavrilă Ogoranu, a fascist leader from the interwar period, still has a statue honouring him in downtown Deva.

The obsession with anti-communism has not receded in political and intellectual life over the past three decades. There are many among the younger generations of urban and foreign educated inhabitants who have moved on from this dominant trope. The superb documentary *Collective*[11] is a great example of what happens when one moves beyond this obsession and judges governance on the basis of contemporary institutions and aspirations toward transparency and serving the common good without bias and "lies told for power and for profit."

But some prominent Romanians have remained enamoured with the notion that anti-communism is a crusade, just as the fascists stated in the 1940s. And some prominent academics, starting with the President of the Romanian Academy, Ioan Aurel Pop, have begun to combine this façade of anti-communism with discursive tropes close to the fascism of Ogoranu. A tribalist view of the Romanian family and society has gained increasing prominence in the public pronouncements of the President of the Academy, and accusations of cosmopolitism and globalism as forms of totalitarian control, equating them with communism and as Soros infiltrators, have started to slide towards essentialist fascist tropes.

A little over a decade ago, Sorin Lavric, then a rising star in the Romanian intellectual scene, won a major prize from the Romanian Academy for a study that was hailed as nuanced, balanced, and profound in its insights.[12] It was a book dedicated to understanding the relationship between Constantin Noica, a prominent philosopher who participated in the fascist movement, and the Legion of the Archangel Michael. A number of scholars criticized the book for its "balanced" view of the legionary movement, whose magnetism Lavric seems to go out of his way to explain in ways that suggest sympathies with the movement. And yet the book was also defended by many scholars in Romania and some overseas, where it was praised without reservation by other experts on "moderation."

Since December 2020, Lavric has become an open apologist for antisemitic, racist, misogynist, and anti-vaccine views espoused by the Alliance for Romanian Unification (aur) party with which he has chosen to affiliate as a stepping stone towards a seat in the Senate. He now promises to start a war that will do away with the current political class. Lavric's party was proud to declare in December that they fully supported Trump, at a time when the President was challenging the democratic outcomes of the US election. More recently, one analysis described Lavric as a "known apologist for Romanian fascism."

The surfacing of fascist sympathies may have been facilitated by Trump, but they represent an older current that has gathered strength from the praises and general acceptance of such perspectives as part of the mainstream of scholarly production or cultural life. There is no reason to believe they will now subside. Trump is gone, but Lavric continues to publish in a prominent weekly literary journal and to participate in political life. In the US, the Charlottesville community has drawn a line in the sand and stated that, in dealing with Trump and the January 6th insurrection, accountability and justice have to precede unity. In Romania, accountability survives like a potted orchid, in small curated spaces, like documentary films.

Brian Hughes, Associate Director at the Polarization and Extremism Research and Innovation Lab (peril) at American University

Debates over the fascist merits of Trumpism have tended to concentrate on four conditions of dispute: 1) Trumpism's ambitions versus 2) its achievements 3) as a political-institutional regime and 4) as a cultural movement. The most heated debates seem to move effortlessly across these sectors, sometimes speaking past one another, sometimes resolving into antimonies of reason, in which either argument appears correct enough on its own merits yet remains incapable of either disproving or reconciling its opposition. I propose that these categories can be usefully realigned in Lacanian terms, which may help to resolve these antimonies. According to such a realignment, debate related to ideology and policy would belong to the register of the Symbolic. Here one might consider immigration under Trump, its continuities with Obama-era policy, and its function to create a class of Muslims and nonwhite Hispanics as homo sacer/the enemy within. Alternatively, debates best sorted into the register of the Real would be those concerning the inarticulable horror (or its absence) of actual events in the Trump presidency. Here one considers the forced rendition of protesters or the mass libidinal discharge of a Trump rally.

And here the Lacanian realignment exposes a critical gap in the preceding debates, that is, a tendency to neglect the register of the Imaginary. One may speculate as to why this is so. It seems that in debates which pit political scientists and historians against themselves and one another, media theorists have (for whatever reason) largely abstained. Yet media images offer a rich vein of evidence pointing to the fascistoid character of the Trumpist Imaginary. Consider the "God Emperor" meme, which portrayed the president as a golden-haired cyborg messiah from the fantasy wargame Warhammer 40k. This image appeared 9,602 times from 2015–2019 on 4chan alone. Or we might turn to the cartoons of Ben Garrison, where Trump is depicted as a smirking trickster with a bodybuilder's physique. More prosaically, we might consider the image of Trump as reality tv star and hero of his own autobiographies: an omnipotent captain of industry. Here we encounter not Trump the man but Trump the image—a fantasy ideal ego which his followers yearn to reflect. In the register of the Imaginary, where the Ur-capitalist god emperor resides, Trump not only meets the criteria of charismatic strongman proposed by Paxton and Payne, he exceeds them. In the capacity of a cosmic messiah, he not only meets the palingenetic criteria set forth by Griffin, he transcends them.

Of course, this does not resolve debates pertaining to the registers of the Symbolic and Real, but it does inform them. The Lacanian triad is inextricably linked and mutually influencing. Thus, questions of policy cannot be considered absent consideration of image, as the desires of the Symbolic proceed from the demands of the Imaginary. Nor can the horrors of the Trumpist Real be considered absent their Imaginary counterparts, as the needs (met or unfulfilled) that suffuse our experience of the Real provide the ground on which the fantasy figures of the Imaginary stand. By reorienting and expanding the question of Trumpism's fascist merits, we may yet do justice to this largely neglected—yet crucially important—dimension of the debate.

Roger Griffin, Emeritus Professor, Oxford Brookes University

In many areas the gulf between academic and media knowledge—especially social media knowledge—resembles Africa's Great Rift Valley. Ever since Trump first exchanged the studios of reality tv for the world of surreality politics the word "fascism" has hovered around his personal style of presidency like pesky midges. Constantly reached for by bloggers and journalists, their persistent use of it unwittingly blurs important differences between non-revolutionary and genuinely revolutionary forms of the far right when characterizing Trump's particular brand of populism. To make matters worse it has been sanctioned in the US by some high-profile academics such as Jason Stanley, Sarah Churchwell, Enzo Traverso and Federico Finchelstein.

Since the 1990s, a growing consensus has emerged within "liberal academia" that fascism is a revolutionary form of ultranationalism that is not just driven by the desire to return the nation to an utterly mythical state of former greatness. Instead, it aspires to create a new, totalizing, postliberal, ethnically based national or international order purged of multiculturalism and pluralism. This was a project that Trump was far too simple-minded, racist, impulsive, narcissistic, materialistic, aporophobic (contemptuous of the poor), and Quixotic (not to say mentally unstable and delusional) in his thought processes to undertake. Unlike Mussolini and Hitler, he was far too concerned with self-aggrandizement to be a revolutionary strategist and leader and create the nucleus of a future leadership. Any sort of coherent ideology or political strategy of the sort needed for structural change was beyond him. In a way, to call Trump a fascist is an insult to fascism.

Obviously, other political constituencies saw him as fascist. Movements of the radical left such as Refuse Fascism did, hoping that the prospect of a Republican coup might galvanize the masses into a carrying out a Marxist revolution. Many in the alt-right saw him as one of theirs, an assumption encouraged by Trump's perverse response to the Charlottesville Unite the Right rally and his exhortation to the Proud Boys to "stand by" in the debate with Biden (a request they complied in the Capitol incursion). Certainly, Trump displayed some of the "antis" of fascism: misogyny, xenophobia, Islamophobia, the rhetoric of restoring a lost national greatness, populist appeals to chauvinism: but it was not consistently "ultra-nationalistic," striving to create an organic (and hence ethnically exclusive) national community beyond the limits of democracy in a new order. Instead, his egomania led him to ride slipshod over core

Enlightenment principles such as the separation of powers, due process, transparency, accountability of power, and respect for the letter and spirit of the constitution.

So, what of Trumpism? A rabble made up of so many heterogenous elements from Catholic conservatives and apocalyptic Dispensationalists to survivalists, nra fanatics, neo-Nazis and outlandish QAnon conspiracy theorists (most of whom disbanded once their saviour failed to defeat Biden and condemned the assault on the Capitol a "heinous attack") can hardly be seen as a "movement," let alone a cohesive ideological and political force. Trumpism may be a form of "paranoid right" but not a fascist right. By encouraging the mob to storm the building Trump was being, not a fascist leader, but an "ochlocrat." Yet liberal humanists should take no comfort from Trump's lack of fascist credentials.

By spending four years crowbarring apart constitutional democracy from the liberalism and civil liberties that humanists, secular and religious, have struggled for over two centuries to weld together into "liberal democracy," Trumpism and other forms of identitarian, ethnocentric populism have arguably posed a greater, more insidious threat to the credibility of democracy world-wide and the prospects for a sustainable world order than revolutionary extremism (which could have been efficiently put down by a display of state power). The digital pundits obsessed with Trump's putative fascism would be advised to devote more time to threats to liberal humanism emanating from within the parliamentary spectrum of politics, and perhaps spare a moment to check out the present state of fascist studies before irresponsibly raising spectres of interwar totalitarianism.

Endnotes
1. Robert Paxton, 'I've hesitated to Call Donald Trup a Fascist. Until Now', Newsweek, January 11, 2021, accessed February 21, 2021, https://www.newsweek.com/robert-paxton-trump-fascist-1560652.
2. Martin Kitchen, Fascism (London: Macmillan 1976), 86.

3. Marik Fielitz and Holger Marks, 'Digital Fascism: Challenges for the Open Society in Times of Social Media,' CRWS Working Papers (2019), accessed February 12, 2021, https://escholarship.org/uc/item/87w5c5gp.
4. '"This has everything to do with race from top to bottom" – Prof Timothy Snyder on Capitol siege,' Channel4.com, January 7, 2021, accessed February 12, 2021, https://www.channel4.com/news/this-has-everything-to-do-with-race-from-top-to-bottom-prof-timothy-snyder-on-capitol-siege.
5. Dangerous Speech, accessed February 12, 2021, https://dangerousspeech.org/.
6. Niall Ferguson, ed., Virtual history: Alternatives and Counterfactuals (London: Picador, 1997).
7. ' Week in Fascism #91: Coalition of Fascist and Trumpian Forces Storm Capital,' itsgoingdown.org, January 11, 2021, accessed February 12, 2021, https://itsgoingdown.org/this-week-in-fascism-91-coalition-of-fascist-and-trumpian-forces-storms-capitol/.
8. 'Neither an Insurrection or Revolt: An Anarchist Response to the Permitted Fascist Temper Tantrum,' itsgoingdown.org, January 12, 2021, accessed February 12, 2021, https://itsgoingdown.org/neither-insurrection-nor-revolt-anarchist-response-dc/.
9. Donald J. Trump (@realDonaldTrump), 'Antifa is a Terrorist Organization, stay out of Washington. Law enforcement is watching you very closely!' Twitter, January 5, 2021, https://twitter.com/realDonaldTrump/status/1346583537256976385?ref_src=twsrc^tfw.
10. Nigel Copsey and Samuel Merrill, 'Violence and Restraint within Antifa: A View from the United States,' Perspectives on Terrorism 14, no. 6 (2020): 122–138, https://www.jstor.org/stable/26964730.
11. Alexander Nanau, Collective (2019).
12. Mirel Horodi, 'Un răspuns evaziv al Academiei,' Observator cultural, no. 510, January 28, 2010, accessed April 13, 2021, https://www.observatorcultural.ro/articol/un-raspuns-evaziv-al-academiei/.

A Strain of Nihilism Infected Trump and the MAGA Movement

Ani Kokobobo

Ani Kokobobo is associate professor and chair in the Department of Slavic Languages and Literatures at the University of Kansas, where she teaches Russian literature and culture.

Nihilism was notably cited during US Senate deliberations after rioting Trump supporters had been cleared from the Capitol.

"Don't let nihilists become your drug dealers," exhorted Nebraska Sen. Ben Sasse. "There are some who want to burn it all down. … Don't let them be your prophets."

How else to describe the incendiary rhetoric and grievances that Donald Trump has peddled since November? What else to call the denial of the electorate's will and his deep disdain for American institutions and traditions?

In 2016, I wrote about how Russian novelist Fyodor Dostoevsky had, in his work, explored what happens to society when people who rise to power lack any semblance of ideological or moral convictions and view society as bereft of meaning. I saw eerie similarities with Trump's actions and rhetoric on the campaign trail.

Fast-forward four years, and I believe the warnings of Dostoevsky—particularly in his most most political novel, *Demons*, published in 1872—hold truer than ever.

Although set in a sleepy provincial Russian town, *Demons* serves as a broader allegory for how thirst for power in some people, combined with the indifference and disavowal of responsibility by others, amount to a devastating nihilism that consumes society, fostering chaos and costing lives.

"Dostoevsky warned of the strain of nihilism that infects Donald Trump and his movement," by Ani Kokobobo, The Conversation, January 13, 2021, https://theconversation.com/dostoevsky-warned-of-the-strain-of-nihilism-that-infects-donald-trump-and-his-movement-152807. Licensed under CC BY-ND 4.0 International.

Power For Power's Sake

Before *Demons*, Dostoevsky had been writing a novel about faith, *The Life of a Great Sinner*.

But then a disturbing public trial spurred him in a more overtly political direction. A young student had been murdered by members of a revolutionary group, The Organization of the People's Vengeance, at the behest of their leader, Sergei Nechaev.

Dostoevsky was appalled that politics could be dehumanizing to the point of murder. His focus turned not only to moral questions but also to political demagoguery, which, he argued, if left unchecked, could result in devastating loss of life.

The result was *Demons*. It featured two protagonists: Pyotr Verkhovensky, a former student with no political convictions beyond a lust for power, and Nikolai Stavrogin, a man so morally numb and emotionally detached that he is incapable of purposeful action and stands idly by as violence engulfs his society.

Through these two figures, Dostoevsky tells a broader story about the many flavors of nihilism. Pyotr infiltrates the town's local social circles, recruits a group of disciples to a revolutionary group and spins lies to band them together so they may do his bidding. Pretending to lead a broad movement of international socialism, Pyotr manipulates those around him into committing violent acts and insurrection against the local government. As a result, one woman is crushed by a mob, a mother and her baby die from chaos and neglect and a fire breaks out that kills multiple others.

Different townspeople espouse multiple and contradictory ideologies; none translates into purposeful action. Instead, they merely leave characters whiplashed and susceptible to being instrumentalized by Pyotor, the master manipulator.

The Allure of Feeling Something

But Pyotr would not prevail without the nihilism of Stavrogin, a local nobleman.

Many townspeople see him as a leader with a strong moral compass. Throughout the novel, Pyotr seeks to loop Stavrogin into his quest for power by either doing him favors that corrupt him or hinting that he will install him as dictator once he successfully carries out a revolution.

On some level, Stavrogin knows better: He should be protecting the town and its people. He ultimately fails to do so, out of sheer despondence and because of the emotional appeal of chaos and violence have for him; they seem to jolt him out of the ennui he often appears to feel.

When given the chance to restrain and turn in to the authorities the escaped convict who perpetrates most of the violence in town, Stavrogin captures him only to eventually let him go. "Steal more, kill more," he says to a criminal who has already admitted to killing and stealing. Later, when the political climate gets so heated that it seems an insurrection is imminent, he flees town.

In surrendering his responsibility to serve as a moral guardian, Stavrogin becomes complicit in Pyotr's schemes. He ultimately kills himself—perhaps, in part, out of guilt for his passivity and moral indifference.

Among the two men, Pyotr is the authoritarian figure. And he cleverly insists that members of the revolutionary group break the law together, cementing a loyal brotherhood of criminality.

By contrast, Stavrogin is the novel's empty center, idly standing by while Pyotr incites violence.

He doesn't help Pyotr. But he doesn't stop him, either.

From Nihilism to Annihilation

A range of nihilistic justifications—each successively hollower than the rest—seems to have shaped the violence at the US Capitol.

The homegrown American insurrection lacked any sort of ideological foundation. Most ideas fueling it are negations of persons or facts. The immediate rallying cry of the insurrection was the falsehood that the election was stolen. Beyond denying the will of over 80 million people who voted for Joe Biden, this lie also qualifies not as an ideology, but as an absolute denial of truth.

Other ideas fomenting the insurrection—such as "America first" or "MAGA" and even white supremacy itself—are quintessentially founded on the denial of others, whether they are immigrants, foreign nationals or persons of color.

From what we have learned since, some of Trump's supporters were even imploring him to "cross the Rubicon," a reference to Julius Caesar's initiation of the civil war that eventually transformed Rome into a dictatorial empire, expressing a longing to smash American systems and eviscerate the republic.

The only real purpose that seems to have brought the group together was devotion to Donald Trump, who strikes me as the arch-nihilist in all this, the Pyotr Verkhovensky of this American tragedy. Then there are the other public figures who should have known better, who might have helped stop it all, but couldn't and didn't. Some, like Stavrogin, excused themselves and were silent for far too long, as the lie about the election grew bigger and bigger. And others seemed to outright encourage the lie through formalized objections in Congress last week.

Playacting at revolution at the behest of a man seeking to cling to power, the rioters ultimately only managed only to vandalize the building, though they left five people dead in their wake.

Nonetheless, to act violently on the basis of such fictions—and to transgress against the humanity of others for nothing at all—is perhaps the most nihilistic act of them all.

QAnon Arose to Meet Trump's Conspiratorial Needs

Ethan Zuckerman

Ethan Zuckerman is former director of the MIT Center for Civic Media and an associate professor of the practice in media arts and sciences at MIT. He currently is associate professor of public policy, communication, and information at the University of Massachusetts.

The Grass Valley Charter School in northern California teaches 500 students from kindergarten to eighth grade using principles from Outward Bound and other "active learning" methods. Recently the school has been in the news not because of its pedagogy, but due to the effects of an unusual eruption of unreality.

On May 11, 2019, the school was scheduled to hold its Blue Marble Jubilee annual fundraiser. In the weeks leading up the event, however, school administrators began receiving calls informing them that a "credible source" had issued warnings that the fundraiser would be a target for an unspecified attack. The people calling the school made clear *they* weren't threatening an attack—they were warning the school about events they anticipated after deciphering a tweet from former FBI director James Comey.

Comey had participated in an online meme, #FiveJobsIveHad, which has served as an opportunity for famous people to display their blue collar roots (and, perhaps, reveal answers to commonly asked online security questions). Followers of the QAnon conspiracy knew better than to take Comey's tweet about his past experience as a grocery store clerk at face value. They turned #FiveJobsIveHad into #FiveJihad and read his five jobs as an acrostic spelling "GVCSF," which online sleuths then determined

"QAnon and the Emergence of the Unreal," by Ethan Zuckerman, *Journal of Design and Science*, July 15, 2019, https://jods.mitpress.mit.edu/pub/tliexqdu/release/4. Licensed under CC-BY 4.0 International.

stood for "Grass Valley Charter School Foundation," the hosts of the jubilee. Cue the phone calls from concerned patriots warning the school of the threat to their fundraiser, warnings that led police to urge the school to call off the event, lest someone show up to "protect the school" and cause mayhem. That fear was not entirely unwarranted—in December of 2016, a conspiracy theorist showed up at a Washington, DC, pizza parlor to "self-investigate" a conspiracy theory spread online, and discharged a semi-automatic rifle in the restaurant before being arrested.

It is perhaps too easy to dismiss QAnon as the craziest manifestation of a crazy time in history, when global narratives about the spread of liberal democracy are rapidly reversing, authoritarian nationalism is re-emerging, and every established political norm seems negotiable. By embracing the most bloody and absurd theories with a credulity that's more easily parodied than examined, QAnon makes it hard for us to take them seriously. But it's a mistake to look at the Grass Valley Charter School episode and shrug.

In 2018, *Time* magazine declared "Q" one of the 25 most influential people on the Internet, alongside more recognizable figures like Donald Trump, Kanye West and Matthew Drudge. It's a reasonable argument to make. Q's "drops"—thousands of cryptic posts posted on image boards 4chan and 8chan—have led to countless YouTube videos, podcasts, and an explosion of online and offline writing trying to interpret the utterances of the anonymous "Q Clearance Patriot." In March of 2019, *QAnon: An Invitation to a Great Awakening*, a book written by QAnon followers and supporters, peaked at #2 on Amazon's list of best selling books.

QAnon is interesting not because its predictions of political revolution are correct—they are not. And while some believers in QAnon have been linked to violence—in particular, the former US Marine who held a one-man standoff at the Hoover Dam, armed with an AR-15 rifle, and who referred explicitly to the QAnon conspiracy—threats of violence are not the main reason to pay attention to this community. Instead, QAnon is important because it is a harbinger of things to come.

A movement like QAnon is an inevitable outgrowth of the Unreal, an approach to politics that forsakes interpretation of a common set of facts in favor of creating closed universes of mutually reinforcing facts and interpretations. Whether the QAnon community flourishes as Donald Trump seeks their approval in his quest for a second term or sputters out as their predictions grow ever more fantastical, the dynamics that make QAnon possible are the same dynamics that are reshaping our politics more broadly.

How Is This Conspiracy Theory Different from Other Conspiracy Theories?

QAnon is a big tent conspiracy theory, a meta narrative that knits together contemporary politics and hoary racist tropes with centuries of history behind them. At its core is the idea that all American presidents between John F. Kennedy and Donald Trump have been working with a cabal of globalist elites called "The Cabal" to undermine American democracy and forward their own nefarious agenda. (Predictably, the cabal includes investor/philanthropist George Soros and the Rothschild family, but the theory is more anti-elite than explicitly anti-Semitic.) In all versions of the mythos, the Cabal seeks to destroy American freedom and subjugate the nation to the wills of a world government. In some versions of the mythos, the agenda also includes pedophilia, blood sacrifice, Satanism and other attention-getting transgressions.

Ultimately, QAnon is a hopeful conspiracy theory. "The Storm" is coming. Donald Trump is secretly working in league with Robert Mueller to arrest Hillary Clinton, Barack Obama, and other members of the Deep State who are working to destroy our nation. Sealed indictments have already been filed, and arrests—followed by military trials, and possibly executions—are coming any day now.

In many ways, QAnon behaves the way most conspiracy theories do. Its core appeal is its sense of a master narrative, an explanation for otherwise disturbing and confusing events that assures believers that they understand the big picture in ways non-believers do not. This master narrative gives believers a sense of control over uncontrollable events. QAnon followers continually remind each other to "trust the plan," that Trump and his team have reasons for the steps they are taking, including their decision to reveal their plans only through the Internet's shadiest message boards.

Like all successful conspiracy theories, QAnon is self-sealing. Any objection or disproof can be turned into support for the theory, usually by explaining that information is being withheld to prevent the panic of an unprepared and potentially hysterical public. Thus events that would seem to doom the theory, like the end of the Mueller investigation, are turned into evidence that those behind the conspiracy—Trump and his allies, including the author of the Q drops—are clever beyond our understanding.

Cass Sunstein understands conspiracies as the product of "crippled epistemologies," which accept only a limited set of sources as authoritative. Here, Donald Trump's relentless attacks on the mainstream media have helped constrain the range of sources QAnon supporters are willing to believe, dismissing virtually any conventional journalistic authorities as part of the globalist elite responsible for all societal ills. The authoritative voices in QAnon are those most dedicated to understanding Q's missives.

But QAnon departs from the pattern of conventional conspiracy theories in some novel ways. Traditionally, the audience for conspiracy theories are those who feel marginalized from ordinary politics and are disengaged. Now the most prominent conspiracy proponent is, arguably, the world's most powerful person. Donald Trump returned to political prominence in 2010, promoting the "birther" conspiracy theory speculating that Barack Obama was not a US citizen. Trump surfaced the idea of running for president in 2011, referring specifically to his belief that Obama's presidency was illegitimate due to his citizenship. Since taking office he has relentlessly attacked mainstream media, which is a core actor in QAnon's unreality, and his voluble conflicts with government agencies like the FBI gives apparent support to the idea that he is at war with a "deep state" determined to unseat him.

Furthermore, Trump frequently amplifies conspiracy theorists, including prominent QAnon believers, especially through his Twitter feed. A generous reading of this behavior is that Trump is amplifying anyone who vocally supports his policies, some of whom happen to be conspiracy theorists. Another interpretation, offered by Joseph Uscinski, is that Trump saw conspiracy theorists as an "underserved market" during the primaries for the 2016 election and that Trump continues "dancing with the one who brought him to the prom." More disturbing is the possibility that Trump genuinely sees himself as a victim of forces beyond his control and the chief actor in a battle for the soul and future of a nation. Whether Donald Trump is a conspiracy theorist or a skilled manipulator of conspiracy theorists, the peculiar logic of "deep state" narratives is a shaping influence on his presidency.

The Radically Participatory Conspiracy

Trump's apparent alignment with some of QAnon's ideas isn't the only distinguishing feature of this conspiracy. QAnon may be the first conspiracy to have fully embraced the participatory nature of the contemporary internet.

The core texts of the QAnon movement are a set of more than 3,000 brief messages posted on Internet message boards 4chan and 8chan. These message boards are anonymous, chaotic and ephemeral, all characteristics that would seem to mitigate against the broad transmission of these missives. Why would "Q Clearance Patriot" (the person or persons who claim proximity to Trump and who have detailed understanding of the conspiracy) share valuable insights in such an unlikely venue? Anonymity, of course, as well as a belief that the open-minded denizens of those fora would be readers capable of assembling the "crumbs" dropped by Q. (Q:#6)

The other reason, of course, is that the process of deciphering and interpreting these vague clues is a hell of a lot more interesting than reading the rantings of a paranoid mind. Author Walter Kirn identifies Q as a storyteller who has mastered a fundamental truth of narrative on the internet: "The audience for internet narratives doesn't want to read, it wants to write. It doesn't want answers provided, it wants to search for them." Members of the QAnon aren't just readers of Q's "drops"—they are the "bakers," assembling crumbs into coherent narratives and predictions. And while assembling and re-baking crumbs is unlikely to yield anything culinarily appealing, participation in constructing the Q narrative is clearly a fascinating pursuit for thousands of co-creators.

Q's literary style is one of relentless questioning, demanding that readers fill in the blanks left in the narrative:

> *Where is Huma? Follow Huma.*
> *This has nothing to do w/ Russia (yet).*
> *Why does Potus surround himself w/ generals?*
> *What is military intelligence?*
> *Why go around the 3 letter agencies? (Q:#2)*

The "baking" of Q's crumbs has led to a complex ecosystem that almost resembles Talmudic commentary, with some "researchers" competing to interpret Q's pronouncements and tie them to breaking events in the news. Other researchers are numerologists, linking the "tripcodes" used in Q's posts (tripcodes are a weak form of cryptographic signature designed to allow anonymous posters to link authorship of multiple posts) to thousands of books indexed by Google Books. Q's devotees are incredibly prolific. The leading Q podcasts have published thousands of episodes, and the thousands of videos explaining QAnon routinely register hundreds of thousands of views on YouTube.

Most commentary on the QAnon phenomenon is so quick to denounce the absurdity of the community's obsessions that it fails to consider what's interesting and novel about the movement. A laudable exception are the three authors behind QAnon Anonymous, a Patreon-supported podcast that "chops & screws the best conspiracy theories of the post-truth era." QAnon Anonymous suggests we understand QAnon as fan fiction: "QAnon has a canon, but the canon is basically this coded language of the drops. The tapestry of the story is done by these amateur researchers...it's decentralized storytelling, like thousands of different fanfic threads going on at once with very little to chew on at the center." While we might think this lack of a strong canon would present an obstacle to the strength of QAnon, it actually serves as a strength.

Much as there's a robust online community extending the narrative of virtually any TV show, movie or beloved work of fiction, QAnon's bakers are taking the narrative sketches offered by Q and extending them into a rich and detailed fantasy world. While there's ample fan fiction about well-loved stories like the Harry Potter series or *Star Trek*, many fanfic aficionados choose to extend flawed texts, fixing their shortcomings and amplifying their strengths. It's far more fun to write fanfic for a bad show than for a perfect one, and the narrative put forward by Q on 4Chan and 8Chan is deeply flawed. It is filled with events that haven't transpired and predictions gone wrong. What is perhaps most remarkable about QAnon is how resilient it has been to obvious setbacks, including the inconvenient truth that neither Hillary Clinton nor Barack Obama have been arrested.

The QAnon Anonymous team considers QAnon to be "an improvisational game" where the players compete, "looking for an interpretation that will go viral within the QAnon community." As a result, QAnon bakers are not only co-authors of the narrative, they're proselytisers, both for the broader conspiracy and their particular interpretive frame. We see the same dynamics in antivax, another conspiracy that's having a moment in the sun with the return of measles outbreaks in the US. It is insufficient to be persuaded by the antivax or QAnon movements—those who've joined the movement feel an obligation to share the truth with those who've yet to be enlightened. Those who are most successful in converting others are rewarded with attention, a commodity that is easily convertible into other currencies. Most of the popular QAnon podcasts feature sponsored advertising, notably products like emergency flashlights designed to help listeners survive the social upheavals destined to come about during The Storm. (There is, of course, the inevitable backlash to the commercialization of QAnon, with disaffected movement participants complaining that the conspiracy has been hijacked and is now being exploited for financial gains.)

Participatory Media and the New Normal

The participatory advocacy that QAnons are engaged in is a phenomenon that's grown increasingly common as news media and participatory social media have become inextricably intertwined. In the broadcast model of media, the events of the world were interpreted by a group of professionals who selected a subset of possible narratives to amplify, then delivered them to audiences who had extremely limited channels in which to offer feedback and input. That model has been largely replaced by one in which the audience is a full participant, an essential circulator of information by retweeting, sharing and remixing it. The new centers of power in this ecosystem are discovery engines like Google and Facebook, which rely on feedback from users to determine what stories to feature or ignore. Additionally, the people formerly known as the audience are now creators of content, adding new chapters to existing stories, and telling entirely new stories.

The field of Civic Media understands participation in this process as a key form of civic participation. Much of this participation is laudable, and a positive development for making marginalized issues more visible. The use of participatory civic media was how reports of sexual harassment in Hollywood turned into the #metoo movement, with tens of thousands of women joining Alyssa Milano in portraying the sheer volume of women who had personally been harassed or abused. In the Black Lives Matter movement, participatory media was critical in documenting police violence against protesters, in demanding attention to protests and the reasons behind them, and in framing the issue of police violence against people of color as narrative of civil rights violation that links together individual acts of violence. The emergence of spaces where non-professional individuals can report what's happening in their communities, amplify stories that might have otherwise been missed, and demand attention towards subaltern narratives is, in the main, an enormously positive development for open societies.

But much as QAnon is an understandable consequence of a president who gives credence to conspiracy theories, QAnon is also a predictable outcome of the rise of this new form of participatory civics. The same tools that allow the emergence of narratives that have been subjugated due to racism, sexism and classism allow the emergence of narratives that were previously ignored because they have little overlap with consensus reality.

With revelations about the use of Facebook groups by the Russian Internet Research Agency to create conflicts between groups of Americans and force cleavages within left-wing movements, it's clear that the social media/news loop is being manipulated. What may be more relevant is the fact that these systems are also useful to those acting "in good faith"—i.e., not misrepresenting their identities or intentions—towards horrific ends. The man who killed 50 Muslims at prayer in New Zealand was not fooled by a Russian plot. Instead, he was recruited by online extremists who believe a conspiracy in which Catholics are being intentionally displaced by Muslims in order to destroy aspects of European culture, a narrative not far from the core QAnon mythos.

Because the Internet is for QAnon and extremists as much as it is for #metoo and Black Lives Matter, the conversation spaces around conspiracies are hard to distinguish at a glance from other forms of newsmaking that happen today. Q comments on the events of the day, linking to YouTube videos and threads on Twitter, and a devoted community interprets and spins his/their commentary in a way that's similar to the President of the United States commenting and linking on Twitter, with an army of journalists reacting to his every tweet.

This media landscape is the new normal. Its key characteristic is not mis-, dis- or malinformation. Instead, the key feature is that every assertion has a point of view behind it and is supporting someone's agenda above other possible agendas. Each story reported or ignored, each fact marshaled or forgotten is weaponized. In such a world, Donald Trump's complaint that the media fails to report on the successes of his presidency is not merely whinging. It is the reason why the media is his most potent antagonist and the "enemy of the people," because the reality they report is in direct conflict with the one he is selling. The conflict between Trump's reality and that of the mainstream media leads to the sense that we are no longer arguing a partisan battle over the interpretation of a common set of facts, but over facts from our own realities that both represent and lead inexorably to our own point of view.

I have started to think of this clash of realities as "the Unreal." I don't mean to identify a singular unreality—Trump's, QAnon's, or anyone else's—but to make the point that what's real to you is unreal to someone else. Like conspiracy theories, this is not a new phenomenon. Questions of whether we can share a common reality or whether we will be forever separated by our perceptions and interpretations are the subject of timeless debates in epistemology and phenomenology. What's different now is that these debates have escaped the philosophy classroom and are now infecting every news story and online discussion.

Throughout QAnon is the idea of discovering that our consensus reality is fraudulent, that a darker but truer reality lurks beneath the surface for those brave enough to look for it. QAnons talk about "red pills" and "blue pills," adopting the terms from everyone's favorite mashup of Keanu Reeves and Plato's Cave, the 1999 film *The Matrix*. In the film, Reeves's character is offered a red pill, which will reveal to him the true and horrifying nature of reality, or a blue pill, which will allow him to remain in happy delusion. For QAnons who've taken the red pill, the world of MSM is unreal, designed to deceive and prevent us from seeing the truth. For those who don't take the pill, those in QAnon are simply delusional, incapable of being reached, and residing in an unreality we have no way of influencing or affecting.

(The adoption of the term "red pill" precedes the QAnon movement and reflects an even darker unreality. The term surfaced in the "pickup artist" community, which is an online group of men who believe women want to be subjugated to men and will reward abusive and dominant men who manipulate them in certain ways. For them, redpilling means releasing yourself from the notions of gender equality and feminism and accepting their deeply misogynistic worldview. That QAnon adopted this language is not coincidental—both communities evolved within the dank, fetid swamps of 4chan and 8chan, and there is a non-zero overlap behind the "traditional values" preached by some QAnon patriots and the revanchist anti-feminists of the pickup artist scene.)

Who Benefits from the Unreal?

If Unreality is an emergent feature in today's world, it is worth asking questions about its effects. Who wins and loses in a world of conflicting realities? Some implications are obvious. Political consensus becomes more elusive, because finding a common solution requires accepting a common—or at least compatible—analysis of the situation. Reporting the news is increasingly complicated, as reporters trained to act as neutral conduits are obliged to advocate for their perspective above competing perspectives, a process that may further erode already diminished trust in journalism.

But deeper effects, like who the unreal helps and harms or what sustained exposure to unreality does to us as citizens or as humans, is harder to divine.

Propaganda is a form of unreality—an instrumental unreality created by a state rather than an organically grown unreality, as QAnon appears to be—and we can learn something about the effects of unreality from the history of propaganda. Hannah Arendt argued that one of the goals of totalitarian propaganda was to force us to believe in the manifestly untrue. In declaring our belief in something that we knew not to be true, we showed our allegiance to the leader who put it forward. When the leader would change their mind and alter the reality that we shared, it would be spun as necessary for disinformation purposes. The leader understood why we needed to lie at some moments and reveal the truth in other moments, and in showing our willingness to adopt this reality, we showed ourselves giving up our agency, becoming the equivalent of a dog waiting for a command from his master rather than thinking on his own.

But it is not clear that our contemporary unrealities have been weaponized and directed in the instrumental way in which totalitarian leaders used propaganda in World War II. Our world is characterized by a diversity of communication channels, a choice of different (un)realities, rather than the control of communications sought by dictatorships. A plurality of unreality does not persuade the listener of one set of facts or another, but encourages the listener to doubt everything.

Some actors seem especially comfortable operating in this environment. RT, the Russian state broadcaster, launched its coverage in the United States with a documentary promoting the conspiracy theory that the terror attacks of 9/11 had been an inside job. This theory, not an especially widespread one in the United States, seems an odd way to introduce oneself to a new audience. But RT's slogan, "Question More," reveals the logic behind it. The goal was not to persuade American viewers of a specific conspiracy theory, but instead to persuade viewers that they should question any narrative that they had previously encountered.

A world in which we are constantly questioning is a world that demands endless effort to navigate. It becomes exhausting to follow the news, to understand political developments, to navigate whether a set of facts is believable or is a manifestation of someone's agenda. A logical response to this rise in unreality is to tune out and sit instead on the sidelines. Another response is to cede agency to those who thrive in this climate of unreality, leaders like Putin and Trump, who seem perfectly adapted to this space.

The main byproduct of unreality is doubt, and doubt is dangerous. Doubt makes it difficult to organize—to demand a change—because movements for change require a set of people to agree on a problem and a possible solution. We know from Naomi Oreskes and Erik Conway in *Merchants of Doubt* that the strategies employed by tobacco companies about the harms of their product or oil companies about anthropogenic climate change were not designed to sway audiences to the corporate narrative, but to generate sufficient doubt to paralyze effective action. As long as there is doubt it is difficult to reach consensus and to move forward. The merchants of doubt wield their product like a weapon, and the primary product of unreality is perpetual paralysis.

We have a tendency to assume, especially in academic communities, that the acceptance of unrealities, whether they are those of vaccine skeptics or climate change deniers, are the consequence of poor education or emergent technologies. Robert Proctor and Iain Boal coined the term "agnotology" to refer to the study of culturally induced ignorance or doubt in order to distinguish ignorance that is consciously created from that which occurs naturally. (I am grateful to Danah Boyd for introducing me to Proctor's book with Londa Schiebinger on the topic, which introduced me to the term.) Those who benefit from the stasis caused by imposed doubt are those who are already in positions of power. Those who suffer the most are those who have been excluded from power. In that sense, unreality and the doubt it generates is an inherently conservative force.

What's worse, perhaps, is that many of our responses to the doubt brought about by emergent unreality have been reactionary. In much of the discussion of mis- and disinformation is the thinly disguised desire to return to a world where there's a single authoritative voice, a Walter Cronkite to tell us "That's the way it is." There is an understandable temptation to hand more power over control of speech to platforms like Facebook in the hopes that they'll somehow return us to a mutually shared reality. This is an unlikely scenario given their role in allowing these splits to emerge. The alternative, asking governments to regulate and control speech in online spaces, seems equally unwise.

Before we hand control of speech to Facebook or to Congress to free us from the complications of the Unreal, we would benefit from mapping this space more comprehensively. The goal of this issue of the *Journal of Design and Science* is not to conclusively define the Unreal, but to explore some of its dimensions. The nature of the beast is such that a singular view of the Unreal would always be incomplete, so we should expect these visions to challenge and conflict with one another as much as they mutually reinforce.

Given antecedents in agnotology within the Russian media space, we invited Peter Pomerantsev, a celebrated writer on contemporary Russia, to explore the idea of unreality as a mirror of a society facing a post-ideological world. Pomerantsev argues that understanding the purpose of disinformation is like trying to understand the purpose of art. Propaganda, like art, simply exists. It's just a reflection of the time.

Masha Gessen, professor at Amherst College, author of *The Man Without a Face: The Unlikely Rise of Vladimir Putin*, and contributor to the *New Yorker*, has challenged overly simplistic narratives of Putin as a singular architect of Russian media interventions. In conversation, she and I explore the idea that the unreal can still be corrosive to democracy even if there's no grand plan behind the complex and conflicting forces that lead to Russian strategies in the information space.

Dr. Gregory Asmolov, a scholar of the Russian internet and early career fellow at King's College London's Russia Institute, argues that the participatory affordances of digital networks offer novel opportunities for political manipulation. Relying on his research on the use of social networks in Russia and Ukraine, he explores the idea that manipulations of social media seek to divide friends, breaking alliances and leaving individuals isolated, online and offline.

Dr. Joan Donovan, Director of the Technology and Social Change Research Project at Harvard's Shorenstein Center on Media, Politics and Public Policy, is one of the nation's leading scholars on online disinformation. As someone who has watched the St. Petersburg-based Internet Research Bureau very closely, her essay with colleague Brian Friedberg, examines the power of pseudonymous identities that adopt the persona of oppressed people to capture their voices and power.

Julia Ebner, an Austrian scholar and researcher at the Institute for Strategic Dialogue, whose book *The Rage* is a leading resource on Islamist and far-right extremists in Europe, uses her knowledge of Neo-Nazi organizing online to give us a tour of alternative infrastructure to support speech that quotidian platforms have rejected.

Unreality can also be routine, as Nina Lutz, an MIT Media Lab researcher on computational geometry and computer graphics explores in an essay that examines how makeup can be used to completely transform identity, and how these transformations impact our understanding of real and fake.

Dr. Judith Donath, former MIT Media Lab professor and alumna, researcher at the Harvard Berkman Klein Center for

Internet and Society, author of *The Social Machine*, expands on her current research on signalling theory to explore the idea of the "deep fake" and to examine our relationship with video as an arbiter of truth, arguing that we must move from understanding video as reality to video as testimony.

Pursuing other spaces where the Unreal pokes into our everyday life, entrepreneur, game designer and former MIT Media Lab professor Kevin Slavin looks at how alternative reality games, a space first explored in the late 1990s and early 2000s, may have prefigured some of the fractures in reality we are encountering today.

And finally, Benjamen Walker, whose *Theory of Everything* podcast has long been one of the most prescient and provocative explorations of internet culture, reflects on a recently completed series, "False Alarm," that explored the blurry lines between fact and fiction. What happens to a media maker whose practice skates across reality's boundaries when the shifting of those boundaries becomes a moment of crisis for society at large?

We will be releasing these essays—and hopefully others—in pairs over the summer of 2019 and encouraging readers to react to them online, inviting other scholars in the field to comment specifically, but also taking advantage of this digital platform's affordances to solicit reactions both to our work and to other voices who should be included in the project.

Keeping firmly in mind the idea that progress is possible through this sort of plurality, I want to return to the question that frequently circulates in the QAnon community: Who is Q?

Is Q a dissident intelligent agent in the President's inner circle? A team of agents? Or perhaps President Trump himself? Is he (or she or they) a profit-making operation put together by opportunistic 4Chan trolls? A giant prank that has grown wildly out of control? A real-life role play, or LARP, as some QAnons like to describe it? Is Q a Psyops effort, designed to keep up the spirit of Trump's most ardent supporters as the President struggles to drain the swamp as he promised them he would do? Is Q an international disinformation operation designed to further pull apart the left and the right much as the Internet Research Agency sought to pull apart Black Lives Matter or the LGB community?

The answer: Q is all of this and more. All of this for the simple reason that somewhere, someone believes this interpretation of Q, and is working to impose that reality on the rest of us. This war between realities is the landscape we find ourselves collectively navigating. It is our task to understand how we act as individuals and citizens in a world where the emergent mode of discourse is not to persuade someone of your interpretation of the facts, but to recruit them to your own reality. Our ultimate challenge is not only to navigate this space but, at best, to heal and transform it.

CHAPTER 2

Was Donald Trump Responsible for the Capitol Riot?

Overview: What Trump Said Before the Capitol Riot

Amy Sherman

Amy Sherman is a staff writer with PolitiFact. She previously worked as a staff writer for the Miami Herald *and the* St. Paul Pioneer Press. *A native of Amherst, Massachusetts, she graduated with a history degree from Macalester College.*

In the weeks leading up to the Jan. 6 riot at the Capitol, President Donald Trump repeatedly said he wanted his supporters to fight Congress on accepting the electoral college results that showed Joe Biden won.

"We're going to walk down to the Capitol, and we're going to cheer on our brave senators, and congressmen and women," Trump told his supporters shortly before the Capitol assault. "We're probably not going to be cheering so much for some of them because you'll never take back our country with weakness. You have to show strength, and you have to be strong."

His supporters listened. Thousands of Trump supporters, waving Trump or Confederate flags and wearing MAGA gear, descended upon the Capitol. They overwhelmed law enforcement, pushed past police barricades, and temporarily stopped Congress from counting electoral votes.

Trump's supporters had gathered earlier in the day for the "Save America" rally organized by a group called "Women for America First." Trump allies, including former campaign staffers, helped promote the event, ABC News reported. Trump's White House schedule showed he was to speak at the rally that day.

Some of Trump's fiercest allies also made incendiary statements at the rally. "Let's have trial by combat," said Trump's lawyer Rudy Giuliani, warming up the crowd for Trump.

"A Timeline of What Donald Trump Said Before the Capitol Riot," by Amy Sherman, April 26, 2021. Copyright ©2021 by Poynter, Reprinted by permission. Used with permission.

We looked closely at the words Trump used to urge his supporters to show up and "fight" on his behalf Jan. 6. With Trump's Twitter account permanently suspended, we used archives of his tweets by Factba.se and the Trump Twitter archive.

We contacted spokespersons for Trump and did not get a response.

What Trump Said Before Jan. 6

For months before Election Day, Trump repeatedly told his supporters falsehoods about voting, including that Democrats had "rigged" the election. Trump ramped up the rhetoric after he lost the election, filing court challenges in battleground states trying to get judges to reverse the outcome. After he racked up defeats in court, Trump's tactics turned toward ordering senators to "fight" for him.

".@senatemajldr and Republican Senators have to get tougher, or you won't have a Republican Party anymore. We won the Presidential Election, by a lot. FIGHT FOR IT. Don't let them take it away!" he tweeted Dec. 18.

In December, Trump also issued a battle cry to his supporters broadly, encouraging them to gather on his behalf Jan. 6.

Dec. 12: On the day of pro-Trump rallies in Washington, D.C., Trump tweeted "Wow! Thousands of people forming in Washington (D.C.) for Stop the Steal. Didn't know about this, but I'll be seeing them! #MAGA."

Dec. 12: "WE HAVE JUST BEGUN TO FIGHT!!!" Trump said in another tweet.

Dec. 19: Trump tweeted his praise for a report by his adviser Peter Navarro alleging election fraud: "A great report by Peter. Statistically impossible to have lost the 2020 Election. Big protest in D.C. on January 6th. Be there, will be wild!"

Dec. 26: Trump tweeted: "The 'Justice' Department and the FBI have done nothing about the 2020 Presidential Election Voter Fraud, the biggest SCAM in our nation's history, despite overwhelming evidence. They should be ashamed. History will remember. Never give up. See everyone in D.C. on January 6th."

Dec. 27: "See you in Washington, DC, on January 6th. Don't miss it. Information to follow!" Trump tweeted.

Jan. 1: "The BIG Protest Rally in Washington, D.C., will take place at 11.00 A.M. on January 6th. Locational details to follow. StopTheSteal!" Trump tweeted.

Jan. 1: "January 6th. See you in D.C." Trump tweeted.

Jan. 3: Trump retweeted @JenLawrence21, an organizer of a March for Trump bus tour: "Now we will bring it to DC on Jan 6 and PROUDLY stand beside you!"

Jan. 3: Trump retweeted Amy Kremer, another promoter of the march who said, "We are excited to announce the site of our January 6th event will be The Ellipse in the President's Park, just steps from the White House!"

Jan. 3: Trump retweeted @CodeMonkeyZ: "If you are planning to attend peaceful protests in DC on the 6th, i recommend wearing a body camera. The more video angles of that day the better."

Jan. 4: At a rally in Georgia the day before the Senate runoffs, Trump repeated his grievances about his own election. He spoke about a continued fight, both for himself and the Senate.

"If the liberal Democrats take the Senate and the White House—and they're not taking this White House—we're going to fight like hell, I'll tell you right now," Trump said.

"We're going to take it back," Trump said.

What Trump Said Before the Riot

Trump's final direction to supporters came during his "Save America" rally around noon Jan. 6, when he repeated his Pants on Fire claim that he won.

"Our country has had enough," Trump told his supporters. "We will not take it anymore and that's what this is all about. To use a favorite term that all of you people really came up with, we will stop the steal."

The crowd later chanted: "Fight for Trump! Fight for Trump! Fight for Trump!" Trump thanked them.

Trump praised the crowd for traveling from across the nation and for "the extraordinary love."

"We're gathered together in the heart of our nation's capital for one very, very basic and simple reason: to save our democracy," Trump said.

Trump repeatedly said there was a need to "fight." After he bashed "weak" Republicans and Biden, he said: "Unbelievable, what we have to go through, what we have to go through and you have to get your people to fight. If they don't fight, we have to primary the hell out of the ones that don't fight. You primary them. We're going to let you know who they are, I can already tell you, frankly."

He continued with the fighting metaphors: "Republicans are constantly fighting like a boxer with his hands tied behind his back. It's like a boxer, and we want to be so nice. We want to be so respectful of everybody, including bad people. We're going to have to fight much harder, and Mike Pence is going to have to come through for us. And if he doesn't, that will be a sad day for our country because you're sworn to uphold our constitution. Now it is up to Congress to confront this egregious assault on our democracy."

Trump then invited the crowd to go to the Capitol.

"And after this, we're going to walk down, and I'll be there with you. We're going to walk down. We're going to walk down any one you want, but I think right here. We're going to walk down to the Capitol, and we're going to cheer on our brave senators, and congressmen and women. We're probably not going to be cheering so much for some of them, because you'll never take back our country with weakness. You have to show strength, and you have to be strong."

Trump used the word "peacefully" once at his rally:

"We have come to demand that Congress do the right thing and only count the electors who have been lawfully slated, lawfully slated. I know that everyone here will soon be marching over to the Capitol building to peacefully and patriotically make your voices heard. Today we will see whether Republicans stand strong for integrity of our elections, but whether or not they stand strong for our country, our country. Our country has been under siege for a long time, far longer than this four-year period."

What Trump Said During and After the Riot

By the time Trump finished his speech, crowds had already started to gather outside the Capitol.

Trump never joined them, but did tweet during the afternoon and night and released a video statement.

"Please support our Capitol Police and Law Enforcement. They are truly on the side of our Country. Stay peaceful!" he tweeted at 2:38 p.m. By that point, the mob had already shattered windows as they pushed inside the building.

His video statement repeated false claims about the fraudulent election and said, "We have to have peace. So go home. We love you. You're very special."

He rehashed those themes in his final tweet of the night. It ended with these words: "Remember this day forever!"

Trump's Supporters Undermine His Impeachment Defense
Zoe Tillman

Zoe Tillman is a senior legal reporter with BuzzFeed News and is based in Washington, DC. She covers courts, justice, and the intersection of law and politics.

Former president Donald Trump formally responded Tuesday to the charges filed by House Democrats in his second impeachment, denying that he incited a mob to violently descend on the Capitol building to stop Congress from certifying President Joe Biden's win.

But court records in the 175-plus criminal cases filed so far in connection with the Jan. 6 insurrection reveal that's exactly what at least some of Trump's supporters thought he was directing them to do.

"[T]oday President Trump told Us to 'fight like hell,'" Troy Smocks, a Texas man charged with making threats, posted on Jan. 6 on Parler, quoting Trump's speech to supporters before the insurrection, according to the government's court filings. Smocks appeared to admit to participating in the attack on the Capitol in his posts, although he isn't charged with that; he urged his followers to get weapons and prepare to "hunt" Democrats, tech executives, and others he considered "enemies of Our constitution," writing, "We now have the green light."

"[Trump] said that Our cause was a matter of national security, and that these people behind the massive fraud must be arrested and brought to justice. And that task, falls on the shoulders of We The People.... the American Patriots," Smocks wrote, court documents say. A judge ordered him to be held in jail pending trial, citing his posts on Parler.

"Trump Supporters' Own Explanations for Assaulting the Capitol Are Undercutting His Impeachment Defense," by Zoe Tillman, February 2, 2021. Copyright © 2021 by Buzzfeed. All rights reserved. Used with permission.

Trump's lawyers are contesting the constitutionality of impeaching a former president, as well as disputing whether he really meant it when he had repeatedly told his supporters to "fight."

"It is denied that the phrase 'if you don't fight like hell you're not going to have a country anymore' had anything to do with the action at the Capitol as it was clearly about the need to fight for election security in general, as evidenced by the recording of the speech," Trump's lawyers wrote in his official response papers.

But court filings in many cases showed that the former president's supporters came to Washington spoiling for a fight and that they broadly took calls from Trump and his allies to "stop the steal"—a reference to baseless claims of widespread voter fraud—to be an appeal for violence. Social media posts, FBI interview summaries, and publicly available interviews that prosecutors included in charging papers also lay out the extent to which Trump's supporters were waiting to take orders from him and understood his words as a direction to act.

Robert Bauer, charged with unlawfully entering a restricted area (the US Capitol) and violent entry and disorderly conduct on Capitol grounds, spoke with two FBI agents on Jan. 8. He "reiterated that he marched to the US Capitol because President Trump said to do so," according to his charging papers. The FBI affidavit includes a screenshot of a selfie found on Bauer's phone that shows him and his cousin (and codefendant) Edward Hemenway II, both wearing "Trump 2020" hats, smiling and posing with their middle fingers up inside the Capitol building.

"According to BAUER, after President Trump told the crowd, 'We are going down Pennsylvania Avenue to the Capitol,' the crowd began moving towards the Capitol," an FBI agent wrote in the affidavit.

Robert Sanford, a Pennsylvania man charged with throwing a fire extinguisher at police officers at the Capitol, similarly told the FBI when he was interviewed on Jan. 12 that he was part of a group that "had gone to the White House and listened to President

Donald J. Trump's speech and then had followed the President's instructions and gone to the Capitol."

In charging papers for Kenneth Grayson of Pennsylvania, the FBI quoted a private message that he allegedly sent to an unidentified person on Dec. 23 about his plans to go to DC on Jan. 6 and take direction from Trump. Grayson, who allegedly livestreamed video on Facebook of himself going into the Capitol and who prosecutors believe is a follower of the QAnon mass delusion, is charged with being a restricted area, disorderly and disruptive conduct, and obstructing an official proceeding.

"I'm there for the greatest celebration of all time after Pence leads the Senate flip!! OR IM THERE IF TRUMP TELLS US TO STORM THE F**IN CAPITAL IMA DO THAT THEN! We don't want any trouble but they are not going to steal this election that I guarantee bro!!" Grayson allegedly wrote.

Samuel Fisher, a New York man charged with illegally going into the Capitol and disorderly conduct, wrote in a lengthy post on his personal website dated Jan. 6, apparently before the attack, "Trump just needs to fire the bat signal… deputize patriots… and then the pain comes."

It's too early in most cases for people charged with participating in the insurrection to have had a chance to offer a defense—but in a few court fights over whether defendants should be kept in jail or allowed to go home pending trial, their lawyers have highlighted the connection between Trump's words and the violence at the Capitol. In opposing pretrial detention for Emanuel Jackson, who is charged with assaulting police officers as well as illegally going into the Capitol, his lawyer wrote that "the nature and circumstances of this offense must be viewed through the lens of an event inspired by the President of the United States." A judge ordered Jackson kept in custody.

A judge is scheduled to hear arguments on Feb. 3 on whether to order pretrial detention for Dominic Pezzola, a New York man and member of the Proud Boys identified in videos breaking a window at the Capitol and who the government alleged had instructions at his home to make guns and bombs. In a recent interview, Pezzola's lawyer told Reuters that the "logical thinking" to Trump's supporters was that the president had "invited" them to Washington.

Reuters also noted that during a Jan. 21 court hearing, a lawyer for Riley Williams of Pennsylvania told the judge that her client "took the president's bait and went inside the Capitol." Williams is charged with illegally going into the Capitol as well as stealing or helping to steal a laptop from House Speaker Nancy Pelosi's office; Williams, through her lawyer, has denied any involvement in the theft.

The House voted to impeach Trump for a historic second time on Jan. 13 for inciting the insurrection at the Capitol. A trial in the Senate is expected to begin next week. The Senate voted last week against a Republican attempt to reject the impeachment effort as unconstitutional, which means a trial will take place, but enough Republican members supported the measure that it's unlikely Democrats can win the two-thirds majority needed to convict Trump of high crimes and misdemeanors.

Trump's Own Words and Lack of Action Show Responsibility

Diane Ravitch

Diane Ravitch is a historian of education and research professor of education at New York University.

Hiding from the rioters in a secret location away from the Capitol, House Minority Leader Kevin McCarthy (R-Calif.) appealed to Jared Kushner, President Trump's son-in-law and senior adviser. Sen. Lindsey O. Graham (R-S.C.) phoned Ivanka Trump, the president's daughter.

And Kellyanne Conway, a longtime Trump confidante and former White House senior adviser, called an aide who she knew was standing at the president's side.

But as senators and House members trapped inside the US Capitol on Wednesday begged for immediate help during the siege, they struggled to get through to the president, who—safely ensconced in the West Wing—was too busy watching fiery TV images of the crisis unfolding around them to act or even bother to hear their pleas.

"He was hard to reach, and you know why? Because it was live TV," said one close Trump adviser. "If it's TiVo, he just hits pause and takes the calls. If it's live TV, he watches it, and he was just watching it all unfold."

Even as he did so, Trump did not move to act. And the message from those around him—that he needed to call off the angry mob he had egged on just hours earlier, or lives could be lost—was one to which he was not initially receptive.

"It took him awhile to appreciate the gravity of the situation," Graham said in an interview. "The president saw these people

"What Trump Did During the Insurrection," by Diane Ravitch, Diane Ravitch, January 16, 2021. https://dianeravitch.net/2021/01/16/what-trump-did-during-the-insurrection/. Licensed under CC-BY-NC-ND-3.0 Unported.

as allies in his journey and sympathetic to the idea that the election was stolen."

Trump ultimately—and begrudgingly—urged his supporters to "go home in peace." But the six hours between when the Capitol was breached shortly before 2 p.m. Wednesday afternoon and when it was finally declared secure around 8 p.m. that evening reveal a president paralyzed—more passive viewer than resolute leader, repeatedly failing to perform even the basic duties of his job.

Capitol Police were unable to stop a breach of the Capitol.

The man who vowed to be a president of law and order failed to enforce the law or restore order. The man who has always seen himself as the protector of uniformed police sat idly by as Capitol Police officers were outnumbered, outmaneuvered, trampled on—and in one case, killed. And the man who had long craved the power of the presidency abdicated many of the responsibilities of the commander in chief.

The episode in which Trump supporters rose up against their own government, leaving five people dead, will be central to any impeachment proceedings, critical to federal prosecutors considering incitement charges against him or his family, and a dark cornerstone of his presidential legacy.

This portrait of the president as the Capitol was under attack on Jan. 6 is the result of interviews with 15 Trump advisers, members of Congress, GOP officials and other Trump confidants, many of whom spoke on the condition of anonymity to share candid details.

The day began ominously, with a "Save America March" on the Ellipse devoted to perpetuating Trump's baseless claims that somehow the 2020 election was stolen from him.

Before the president's remarks around noon, several of his family members addressed the crowd with speeches that all shared a central theme: Fight. Eric Trump, one of the president's sons, told the crowd that lawmakers needed to "show some fight" and "stand up," before urging the angry mass to "march on the

Capitol today." Donald Trump Jr., another of the president's sons, exhorted all "red-blooded, patriotic Americans" to "fight for Trump."

Backstage, as the president prepared to speak, Laura Branigan's hit "Gloria" was blared to rev up the crowd, and Trump Jr., in a video he recorded for social media, called the rallygoers "awesome patriots that are sick of the bull----." His girlfriend, Kimberly Guilfoyle, danced to the song and, clenching her right fist, urged people to "fight."

The president, too, ended his speech with an exhortation, urging the crowd to give Republicans "the kind of pride and boldness that they need to take back our country."

"So let's walk down Pennsylvania Avenue," he concluded.

Trump, however, did not join the angry crowd surging toward the Capitol. Instead, he returned to the White House, where at 2:24 p.m. he tapped out a furious tweet railing against Vice President Pence, who in a letter earlier in the day had made clear that he planned to fulfill his constitutional duties and certify President-elect Joe Biden and Vice President-elect Kamala D. Harris as the winners of the 2020 electoral college vote.

"Mike Pence didn't have the courage to do what should have been done to protect our Country and our Constitution, giving States a chance to certify a corrected set of facts, not the fraudulent or inaccurate ones which they were asked to previously certify," he wrote. "USA demands the truth!"

By then, West Wing staffers monitoring initial videos of the protesters on TV and social media were already worried that the situation was escalating and felt that Trump's tweet attacking Pence was unhelpful.

Press officials had begun discussing a statement from Trump around 2 p.m., when protesters first breached the Capitol, an official familiar with the discussions said. But they were not authorized to speak on behalf of the president and could only take the matter to Chief of Staff Mark Meadows, this person

Was Donald Trump Responsible for the Capitol Riot?

said, adding that "the most infuriating part" of the day was how long it took before Trump finally spoke out.

Around the same time, Trump Jr. headed to the airport for a shuttle flight home to New York. As he waited in an airport lounge to board the plane, the president's namesake son saw that the rallygoers they had all urged to fight were doing just that, breaching police barricades and laying siege to the Capitol.

An aide called Trump Jr. and suggested he immediately issue a statement urging the rioters to stop. At 2:17 p.m., Trump Jr. hit send on a tweet as he boarded the plane: "This is wrong and not who we are," he wrote. "Be peaceful and use your 1st Amendment rights, but don't start acting like the other side. We have a country to save and this doesn't help anyone."

But the president himself was busy enjoying the spectacle. Trump watched with interest, buoyed to see that his supporters were fighting so hard on his behalf, one close adviser said.

But if the president didn't appear to understand the magnitude of the crisis, those in his orbit did. Conway immediately called a close personal aide who she knew was with the president, and said she was adding her name to the chorus of people urging Trump to speak to his supporters. He needed to tell them to stand down and leave the Capitol, she told the aide.

Conway also told the aide that she had received calls from the D.C. mayor's office asking for help in getting Trump to call up the National Guard.

Ivanka Trump had gone to the Oval Office as soon as the riot became clear, and Graham reached her on her cellphone and implored her for help. "They were all trying to get him to speak out, to tell everyone to leave," said Graham, referring to the small group of aides with Trump on Wednesday afternoon.

Several Republican members of Congress also called White House aides, begging them to get Trump's attention and have him call for the violence to end. The lawmakers reiterated that they had been loyal Trump supporters and were even willing to vote against the electoral college results—but were now scared for their lives, officials said.

When the mob first breached the Capitol, coming within mere seconds of entering the Senate chamber, Pence—who was overseeing the electoral certification—was hustled away to a secure location, where he remained for the duration of the siege, despite multiple suggestions from his Secret Service detail that he leave the Capitol, said an official familiar with Pence's actions that day. Instead, the vice president fielded calls from congressional leaders furious that the National Guard had not yet been deployed, this official said. Pence, from his secret location in the Capitol, spoke with legislative and military leaders, working to mobilize the soldiers and offering reassurance.

Even as his supporters at the Capitol chanted for Pence to be hanged, Trump never called the vice president to check on him or his family. Marc Short, Pence's chief of staff, eventually called the White House to let them know that Pence and his team were okay, after receiving no outreach from the president or anyone else in the White House. Meanwhile, in the West Wing, a small group of aides—including Ivanka Trump, White House press secretary Kayleigh McEnany and Meadows—was imploring Trump to speak out against the violence. Meadows's staff had prompted him to go see the president, with one aide telling the chief of staff before he entered the Oval Office, "They are going to kill people."

Shortly after 2:30 p.m., the group finally persuaded Trump to send a tweet: "Please support our Capitol Police and Law Enforcement," he wrote. "They are truly on the side of our Country. Stay peaceful!"

But the Twitter missive was insufficient, and the president had not wanted to include the final instruction to "stay peaceful," according to one person familiar with the discussions.

Less than an hour later, aides persuaded Trump to send a second, slightly more forceful tweet: "I am asking for everyone at the US Capitol to remain peaceful," he wrote. "No violence! Remember, WE are the Party of Law & Order—respect the Law and our great men and women in Blue. Thank you! You're very special."

McCarthy did eventually reach Trump, but later told allies that he found the president distracted. So McCarthy repeatedly appeared on television to describe the mayhem, an adviser said, in an effort to explain just how dire the situation was.

McCarthy also called Kushner, who that afternoon was arriving back from a trip to the Middle East. The Secret Service originally warned Kushner that it was unsafe to venture downtown to the White House. McCarthy pleaded with him to persuade Trump to issue a statement for his supporters to leave the Capitol, saying he'd had no luck during his own conversation with Trump, the adviser said. So Kushner headed to the White House.

At one point, Trump worried that the unruly group was frightening GOP lawmakers from doing his bidding and objecting to the election results, an official said.

National security adviser Robert C. O'Brien also began calling members of Congress to ask how he could help. He called Sen. Mike Lee (R-Utah) around 4 p.m., a Lee spokesman said. In an unlikely twist, Lee had heard from the president earlier—when he accidentally dialed the senator in a bid to reach Sen. Tommy Tuberville (R-Ala.) to discuss overturning the election.

Others were still having trouble getting through to the White House. Speaking on ABC News shortly before 4 p.m. Wednesday, Chris Christie, a GOP former governor of New Jersey, said he'd spent the last 25 minutes trying to reach Trump directly to convey a simple, if urgent, message.

"The president caused this protest to occur; he's the only one who can make it stop," Christie said. "The president has to come out and tell his supporters to leave the Capitol grounds and to allow the Congress to do their business peacefully. And anything short of that is an abdication of his responsibility." Around this time, the White House was preparing to put out a video address on behalf of the president. They had begun discussing this option earlier but struggled to organize their effort. Biden, meanwhile, stepped forward with remarks that seemed to rise to the occasion: "The scenes of chaos at the Capitol do not reflect the true America, do not represent who we are."

Trump aides did three takes of the video and chose the most palatable option—despite some West Wing consternation that the president had called the violent protesters "very special."

"This was a fraudulent election, but we can't play into the hands of these people," Trump said in the video, released shortly after 4 p.m. "We have to have peace. So go home. We love you. You're very special. You've seen what happens. You see the way others are treated that are so bad and so evil. I know how you feel. But go home, and go home in peace."

Amid the chaos, D.C. Mayor Muriel E. Bowser (D) had implemented a 6 p.m. curfew for the city, and as darkness fell, the Secret Service told West Wing staff that, save for an essential few, everyone had to leave the White House and go home.

At 6:01 p.m., Trump blasted out yet another tweet, which Twitter quickly deleted and which many in his orbit were particularly furious about, fearing he was further inflaming the still-tense situation.

"These are the things and events that happen when a sacred landslide election victory is so unceremoniously & viciously stripped away from great patriots who have been badly & unfairly treated for so long," Trump wrote. "Go home with love & in peace. Remember this day forever!"

Thirteen minutes later, at 6:14 p.m., a perimeter was finally established around the Capitol. About 8 p.m., more than six hours after the initial breach, the Capitol was declared secure.

The following evening, on Thursday, Trump released another video, the closest advisers say he is likely to come to a concession speech. "Congress has certified the results: A new administration will be inaugurated on January 20th," Trump said in the video. "My focus now turns to ensuring a smooth, orderly, and seamless transition of power. This moment calls for healing and reconciliation."

His calls for healing and reconciliation were more than a day too late, many aides said. Yet as Trump watched the media coverage of his video, he grew angry. The president said he wished he hadn't done it, a senior White House official said, because he feared that the calming words made him look weak.

Social Media Bears Some of the Blame for the Riot
Erika D. Smith

Erika D. Smith is a columnist for the Los Angeles Times *who writes about the diversity of people and places across California. She previously worked at the* Sacramento Bee, *where she was a columnist and editorial board member covering housing, homelessness, and social justice issues.*

There is plenty of blame to go around for why a MAGA-outfitted mob felt bold enough to break into the US Capitol on Wednesday. President Trump and his Republican enablers are at the top of the list, but several California social media companies aren't too far behind them.

Twitter. Facebook. Instagram. YouTube. Google.

For years, the executives of these companies have known that their platforms serve as convenient breeding grounds for dangerous, right-wing conspiracy theories.

Remember when former President Obama warned Facebook founder Mark Zuckerberg that fake news was being on spread on Facebook and would influence the 2016 election and he dismissed it as "crazy"?

Remember Pizzagate, when a North Carolina man armed himself with a rifle and drove hundreds of miles to rescue children he believed were supposedly trapped in a sex-slave ring run out of a Washington pizzeria by a cabal of Democrats?

I do. Yet, somehow these executives—their fortunes reliant on people spending as much time in their online ecosystems as possible—haven't done a whole heck of a lot to rid their platforms of such conspiracy theories that lead to real-world consequences. And

"Column: It is Not Just Trump. Blame California Social Media Companies for D.C. Riot Too," by Erika D. Smith, *LA Times,* January 7, 2021. Reprinted by permission.

this is in spite of the many grillings they've received by members of Congress, the last one in October.

What happened at the US Capitol, with rioters disrupting the normally peaceful transfer of power between presidential administrations, can in many ways be traced back to the lack of urgency over such situations from social media companies.

For days leading up to the electoral college vote tally, Trump's supporters had been talking about violence, several experts said on Wednesday. There were threats against elected officials and police officers, and talk of a second civil war from everyone from the "boogaloos" to self-styled militia groups.

Meanwhile—both inexplicably and predictably—Trump's supporters have been taking to Twitter and Facebook to blame antifa for raiding the Capitol.

"We are seeing significant volumes of rhetoric online," Daniel Jones, president of Advance Democracy, told USA Today. "And we're seeing this rhetoric—fueled by President Trump's voter fraud claims—across all social media platforms."

As of Wednesday afternoon, President Trump still had an active Facebook account from which he could spread even more inflammatory lies to rile up his increasingly desperate base of crazies.

The company announced later that evening that it would block his ability to post for 24 hours—an unprecedented step but still basically a slap on the wrist.

And then on Thursday morning, Zuckerberg finally came to his senses and announced that Facebook would suspend Trump's account through the end of his presidency.

"We believe the risks of allowing the President to continue to use our service during this period are simply too great," Zuckerberg wrote in a Facebook post. "Therefore, we are extending the block we have placed on his Facebook and Instagram accounts indefinitely and for at least the next two weeks until the peaceful transition of power is complete."

Trump still has a Twitter account, though. After most of the MAGA people had already been cleared from the Capitol, the company said it would lock the president out of his account for 12 hours and warned that he could be booted off the platform permanently.

Also, late Wednesday, both Twitter and Facebook took the rare step of removing a video in which Trump, under pressure, half-heartedly called for his supporters to be peaceful, but added in a bunch of other nonsense about Democrats and the election supposedly being stolen.

Why did it take an attempted coup for Twitter and Facebook to act? And why does the outgoing president still have an account at all?

For weeks, he has been spreading conspiracy theories about how the election was "rigged" and how ballots were being "found" under tables. He's been attacking election workers and Democrats by name as part of the "deep state."

As a result, Twitter has been labeling many of the president's recent tweets as inaccurate, but not removing them—as if that was supposed to persuade someone that Trump was lying.

Republican Sen. Ben Sasse of Nebraska had it right when he tweeted that the Capitol "was ransacked while the leader of the free world cowered behind his keyboard—tweeting," and that Wednesday's "violence was the inevitable and ugly outcome of the president's addiction to constantly stoking division."

It's also the inevitable and ugly outcome of social media companies leaving conspiracy theories to fester and spread online.

Anyone who has been to a Trump rally over the past four years—as I unfortunately have—can attest to the fact that attendees speak a different language of convoluted falsehoods. It's like going to a "Star Trek" convention without ever having seen an episode of "Star Trek" and trying to have a conversation with a Romulan and a Klingon.

Even without the president repeating conspiracy theories and egging people on from Twitter, these tall tales spread like wildfire online. And they can turn particularly dark in less populated, less regulated corners of the web, such as Parler, which will undoubtedly draw more followers if Twitter and Facebook finally crack down.

Whatever California's social media companies have done to stem the tide of disinformation clearly isn't enough. We can't afford more online violence seeping into the real world.

Ex-Delaware Attorney General Says Trump Is Not Responsible for Capitol Siege

Meredith Newman, Ryan Cormier, and Sarah Gamard

Meredith Newman, Ryan Cormier, and Sarah Gamard work for the Delaware News Journal. Newman covers health care in Delaware, and, recently, the presidential run of Joe Biden. Cormier writes about pop culture and entertainment. Gamard primarily covers state government.

The leader of the Delaware Republican Party said she believes President Donald Trump is not responsible for the violent mob that stormed the Capitol last week—and should not be removed from office.

"I don't think he committed any act that would warrant impeachment under the law, as the law is comprised, candidly," said GOP Chairwoman Jane Brady, who is also a former state attorney general and Superior Court judge. "If you listen to (Trump's) whole speech, you would see that as well."

While Brady described the siege of the Capitol as "horrible" and an "attack on our democracy," she did not call it an insurrection or an act of domestic violence. She compared the events of Jan. 6 to the Black Lives Matter protests—which called for racial justice—saying that peaceful protests were not responsible for the looting and violence of a "few criminal people."

Yet the mob consisted of thousands of people, many of whom were armed with weapons, ransacked congressional offices and threatened the lives of House Speaker Nancy Pelosi and Vice President Mike Pence—all while Congress was in the process of certifying the presidential election.

"Ex-Delaware Attorney General Says Trump Not Responsible for Capitol Siege," by Meredith Newman, Ryan Cormier and Sarah Gamard, Delawareonline.com, January 15, 2021. Reprinted by permission.

The death toll from the mob attack has reached five, including two Capitol Police officers.

Brady, who ran unsuccessfully against President-elect Joe Biden for his Senate seat in 1990, was one of several Delaware Republicans who expressed support for the president despite many viewing him as inciting the violent mob and then failing to act when rioters invaded the Capitol.

As the country braces for the possibility of more armed protests at US and state capitols in the coming days, other Republican politicians in Delaware lamented the violence of Jan. 6 while also defending the president. Delaware Republicans say they are not aware of any plans for protests in Dover this weekend.

"We've experienced four years of total persecution of the man who was elected to be our president," said Rep. Rich Collins, R-Millsboro. "And I, frankly, am not surprised that people are angry."

US House Democrats on Monday introduced an article of impeachment against the president for inciting the mob. Delaware's congressional delegation—Rep. Lisa Blunt Rochester and Sens. Tom Carper and Chris Coons—support Trump's removal.

As he headed to Texas on Tuesday, Trump called the second impeachment efforts against him a "witch hunt" and expressed no remorse for inciting the violence.

On Wednesday, Trump, charged with "incitement of insurrection," was impeached by the US House for a historic second time by a vote of 232-197.

The chaos at the Capitol began just after Trump spoke to a crowd of thousands at a Jan. 6 rally near the White House. He repeatedly told his supporters to "fight" during his speech and then told them to march to the Capitol.

What then unfolded was one of the darkest days in the country's history. The mob made its way with relative ease into the Capitol, where Congress was certifying the results of the presidential election.

The rioters attacked officers with "metal pipes, discharged chemical irritants" and other weapons, according to US Capitol Police. Some of these rioters carried loaded handguns and wore bulletproof vests and other military-style gear. Many wore insignia for extremist, far-right militia groups. Molotov cocktails were found in the area.

One man was seen in black paramilitary-type clothing, carrying plastic zip ties that are sometimes used for restraint. This Tennessee man was one of many rioters to be arrested in the days that followed the insurrection.

All the while, members of Congress, their staff and journalists sheltered in place, fearing for their lives, as the mob destroyed some offices.

Since the assault on the Capitol, a swelling number of lawmakers have blamed Trump for inciting this violence and called for him to be removed from office. Two Republican senators—Pat Toomey of Pennsylvania and Lisa Murkowski of Alaska—joined Democrats in calling for the president to resign over the riot.

Brady said six buses of Trump supporters traveled to Washington for the president's rally. She said the Republican Party did not organize or pay for the buses but provided information to Republican voters. Brady said she was not aware of anyone from the buses involved in any investigation regarding the event at the Capitol.

On Thursday, Laurel residents Kevin Seefried and his son, Hunter, were arrested and appeared in federal court in Wilmington to face charges stemming from the Capitol insurrection.

The two face multiple federal charges including entering a restricted building, as well as violent entry and disorderly conduct on Capitol grounds. Court documents indicate that Hunter Seefried additionally faces charges of destroying government property.

Brady said the Seefrieds were not on the six buses to Washington that day.

Brady said she doesn't regret providing information about the rally because people went to support the president. She still maintains that election "irregularities" occurred as a result of mail-in voting, but did not provide any evidence.

Contrary to Trump's false claims, there is no evidence of widespread election fraud.

Some of the Republican state lawmakers said it is still unclear who was at fault for the violence.

Rob Arlett, the state's 2016 Trump campaign chair, believes members of Antifa or Black Lives Matter were inside the Capitol that day despite there being no evidence backing these claims.

He defended Trump, saying that the president denounces violence and has been "very consistent and very vocal about peaceful protests."

"Now, all of a sudden, the Trump supporters are the ones who are full of hate?" Arlett said. "I beg to differ. We're not."

Sen. Dave Lawson, R-Marydel, expressed sadness for Wednesday's events.

"The loss of life is absolutely deplorable," Lawson said. "There was no reason for it."

He said the rioters' ability to easily break into the building and into House Speaker Nancy Pelosi's office "raises suspicion."

"In reality, it is the people's house," Lawson said. "They have the right to access it. They don't have the right to destroy it."

Former Delaware Gov. and US Rep. Michael Castle said he found the incident at his former workplace of 18 years "unbelievable."

He laid much of the blame on the rioters.

"I don't care what Trump may have said in his speech or anything else—they had to know they were in violation of the law when they were destroying property and disrupting the business of Congress," he said. "They went far beyond anything I could have imagined."

Castle did not support Trump in the Republican primary but did vote for him in the 2016 general election. He has been critical of him at times and now believes Trump's political power has been greatly weakened by the riot.

Castle, who lost his 2010 Republican US Senate primary to conservative activist Christine O'Donnell, has come face to face with conspiracy theories himself. Most notably at a 2009 town hall meeting when a woman broke down in tears demanding to see President Barack Obama's birth certificate.

"He is a citizen of the United States," Castle told her over loud boos and yelling in the crowd, a video of which went viral.

The moderate Republican, now 81, sees a connection between moments like that and what happened in Washington on Jan. 6. Conspiracies abound in both cases. And it was even an outspoken TV personality, O'Donnell that caused Castle's "political demise," as he now calls it.

Back then, the rift in the Republican Party was caused by the tension between the establishment and the tea party movement. The party has since tilted right under Trump, both nationally and in Delaware. Lauren Witzke, the QAnon-friendly 2020 US Senate candidate who lost to Coons, is cited by Castle as an example of the change.

"The Republican Party has strayed pretty far from the days of Pete du Pont as governor or Bill Roth as our senator," he said.

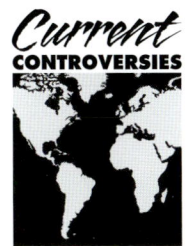

CHAPTER 3

Should Those Who Stormed the Capitol Be Harshly Punished?

Overview: The Capitol Riots Provided America with a Teachable Moment

Scott Shackford

Scott Shackford is an associate editor at Reason. He covers tech surveillance and privacy, criminal justice reform, LGBT issues, and national security policies. He was formerly editor in chief of the Desert Dispatch *in Barstow, California.*

Much of America came to a screeching halt on Wednesday as supporters of President Donald Trump, driven by unfounded conspiracy theories that the election had been stolen and unwilling to accept his defeat, invaded the US Capitol, shattering windows, storming congressional offices, and fighting with police.

Words like insurrection, sedition, and domestic terrorism were tossed about with angry abandon. Many noted that the Capitol Police seemed a lot more careful and polite about getting the angry mob out of the building than law enforcement in general treated Black Lives Matter protesters in Washington, D.C., though police did shoot and kill an unarmed woman during Wednesday's riot. Arrests were few during the incident itself. Afterward, the FBI began to search out people who participated in the trespassing and vandalism for prosecution. Many more arrests followed.

While it's abundantly clear that America is deeply embedded in a populist culture war, it's dangerous to respond to emotion-driven criminal behavior with emotion-driven legal enforcement. After a year of calls to reform America's policing so that officers don't respond to every problem with violence and to reform our justice system so that we don't lock people up for long periods of time unnecessarily, now is not the time to backslide into bad habits.

"What Should Happen to the Capitol Invaders?" by Scott Shackford, January 8, 2021. Copyright © 2021 by Reason.com and Reason magazine. Reprinted by permission.

The desire to "make examples" out of people charged with crimes out of the belief that this deters future criminals has long contributed to America's extremely high incarceration rate. And yet, as we see with incredibly harsh mandatory minimum sentences as part of America's drug war, the cure is often crueler than the crime and is not particularly effective in controlling people's behavior.

In a country that values liberty, what does "justice" look like for the men and women who trespassed in the US Capitol? We should consider what's appropriate on the basis of the reforms some Americans have been pushing for years.

Limit Pretrial Detention to Those Who May Be Planning More Crimes

America has a pretrial detention problem. We have half a million people who are behind bars who have not yet been convicted of a crime. This is, fortunately, much less common on the federal level, where there are fewer than 50,000 people being detained prior to trial (this isn't counting immigration holds).

Pretrial detention is intended to be used when there's no other option to make sure defendants show up for court dates or prevent them from committing other crimes while awaiting trial. But the reality is that our justice system has been throwing people in jail because they couldn't afford bail requirements or because prosecutors exaggerate dangers, and then apply pressure on defendants to accept plea deals so that they hopefully stop languishing in jail. Pretrial detention has turned justice on its head by punishing citizens before they've been convicted.

We are also in the midst of a pandemic that has hit jails and prisons hard. We do not need to be filling up jail cells with people who, emotional responses aside, were acting out a deluded fantasy and are likely not an imminent threat. Throughout 2020, Reason covered prisons' mishandling of the COVID-19 pandemic and the deaths that followed. Twenty percent of the prison population across the country has been infected with the virus.

And in this case, given that the rioters weren't exactly following pandemic safety protocols, the risk here is that these people may bring COVID-19 into jail with them, potentially exposing guards and other inmates.

Seek Restitution, Not Jail Time, Whenever Possible

The damage to the US Capitol can be repaired. The responses to the Capitol invasion have echoed reactions to violence and looting that cropped up during Black Lives Matter protests, heavily fueled with whataboutism. Some see media quick to tar all these participants as threats to public order while dismissing the violence and destruction that took place over the summer. Others see police treating these angry white folks a lot more nicely than they do protesting minorities, even attempting to justify the behavior of the vandals.

To the extent that these claims are true, they represent ongoing cultural criminal justice concerns that are part of reform efforts. The Justice Department's response to crimes that took place in the Capitol should align with these efforts to make America a country that incarcerates at far lower rates than it does now.

Resist the urge to pile on more crimes based on a sense of outrage. The US Capitol is not, in fact, some sort of sacred, unsullied fortress. It's a big building that serves as one of many laboratories of democracy. It should not be treated as somehow more valuable under the law because of what takes place in the building. It's the people that make democracy function, not architecture.

For those responsible for organizing and encouraging violence, those who apparently planted pipe bombs, and those who directed their violence toward other human beings (not buildings), tougher penalties should apply, but we should still, when possible, strive for restitution rather than incarceration, making them pay for the costs of setting things right, repair or replace what was vandalized, and cover the medical care of anybody they injured. Federal prison terms should be considered for those we believe will continue to attempt to cause harm or try to foment further violence if they remain free.

Hold People Responsible for What They Did, and Only What They Did

On Thursday evening, Capitol Police announced that an officer on the scene, Brian Sicknick, had died of injuries he had received while trying to respond to the assault on the Capitol building.

The response to Sicknick's death brought out some of the worst instincts of Twitter users, with some people saying that anybody who participated in the invasion of the Capitol should be held accountable for the man's death.

Take note of this tweet from Rep. Ted Lieu (D–Calif.) on his personal account:

> Every single #MAGA rioter who committed a felony in relation to the death of the US Capitol police officer can charged with felony murder.
> Also, @realDonaldTrump needs to resign immediately.
> —Ted Lieu @tedlieu 2:03AM Jan 8, 2021

He's referring to the rule of felony murder, a legal doctrine that allows prosecutors to charge a person with murder if somebody dies during the commission of a felony, even if the offender played no role in the person's death and did not intend for anybody to die.

The felony murder rule is terrible. It's not justice. It should be eliminated. We should not be convicting people of murder when they did not, in fact, commit murder. I bring up Lieu's tweet here because California, the state he represents, mostly eliminated its own version of the felony murder rule in 2018 (though it is worth noting that killing a police officer remains its most significant exception, and so it would still apply here if this all took place in California).

There are many, many penalties we can throw at these people, and federal prosecutors habitually charge defendants with any possible violation they can unearth in order to intimidate them into plea bargains. The only people we should consider charging with murder are those who are actually responsible for Sicknick's injuries.

We Have Enough Laws to Address This Invasion and Don't Need More

There have been dozens of arrests related to the assault on the Capitol. Everything any of these people did that harmed a person or property at the Capitol is a violation of an existing law.

It feels important to point this out because, in the wake of any outrage-inducing criminal event, politicians will quickly come forth to try to take advantage of the situation to introduce laws to make the government more powerful and increase the punishment and incarceration of citizens.

President-elect Joe Biden says he is open to passing more laws to address domestic terrorism, possibly including "red flag laws" that allow the government to forbid citizens from possessing guns even if they haven't been convicted of crimes out of fear of what they might do.

If Trump's presidency has taught us anything at all, it should be that the federal government is extremely powerful. What happened on Wednesday is a result of poor planning and police control, not a result of the government not being powerful enough to stop it.

Fox News pointed out that these trespassers could face long federal prison sentences thanks to Trump's call to prosecute anybody damaging federal monuments, an executive order he put in place to go after antifa members.

Nobody should face 10 years in federal prison for breaking windows, or stealing a bust, or destroying chairs. That's not a proportionate response. That's anger and disgust channeled through the halls of authority, not justice. It will not create peace. It will create martyrs. It won't prevent future violence—it will foment it.

Make Sure These People Are Aware of The Mercies Extended to Them

There is an irony, of course, that many of these same people believe in the same extremely harsh forms of justice that Trump does. They see antifa everywhere. Some cynically attempted to blame the invasion on antifa. They refuse to accept the harshness of the criminal justice system because they aren't typically the targets.

Resist the instinct to "teach them a lesson" by making them the targets. But do make sure they know exactly what could have happened. Make sure they know that it's only because of the activism of the very criminal justice reformers they dismiss that they're not being treated the way the federal government treated criminals in the 1990s.

Most Americans Want the Rioters Prosecuted
Pew Research Center

Pew Research Center is a nonpartisan fact tank that informs the public about the issues, attitudes, and trends shaping the world. They conduct public opinion polling, demographic research, content analysis and other data-driven social science research. They do not take policy positions.

As the FBI and other federal law enforcement agencies continue to pursue charges against participants in the Jan. 6 riot at the US Capitol, the American public generally expresses strong support for continuing these efforts. Yet there are sizable partisan differences in attitudes about the riot at the Capitol, with Democrats far more likely than Republicans to view prosecution of the rioters as very important and to say that penalties for the rioters are likely to be less severe than they should be.

The survey by Pew Research Center, conducted March 1-7, 2021, among 12,055 US adults who are members of the Center's nationally representative American Trends Panel, finds a wide majority of Americans (69%) saying it is "very important" for federal law enforcement agencies to find and prosecute the people who broke into the US Capitol on Jan. 6. Another 18% say doing this is "somewhat important." Just 12% say this is not too or not at all important.

Nearly half of Americans (47%) say the criminal penalties that the rioters will receive are likely to be less severe than they should be given what happened, while 22% say the penalties will be more severe than they should be. Only about three-in-ten (29%) expect the punishments will be about right.

"Large Majority of the Public Views Prosecution of Capitol Rioters as 'Very Important,'" Pew Research Center, March 18, 2021. Reprinted by permission.

Should Those Who Stormed the Capitol Be Harshly Punished?

The public generally expresses confidence in federal law enforcement agencies to find and prosecute those who broke into the Capitol on Jan. 6. Still, of those who say it is important for these agencies to complete this task, only 20% have a "great deal" of confidence that law enforcement will bring the rioters to justice, while another 48% have a "fair amount" of confidence.

Republicans and Democrats differ sharply over how important it is for law enforcement to prosecute those involved in the Jan. 6 riots and whether criminal penalties will be less severe than deserved. Partisans are less divided over whether federal law enforcement agencies are up to the task of finding and prosecuting participants who scattered across the country after the events that day.

While large majorities in both parties (95% of Democrats and 79% of Republicans, including those who lean to each party) say it is at least somewhat important that federal law enforcement agencies find and prosecute those responsible for the Jan. 6 riot, Democrats are more intense in their views: Fully 86% of Democrats and independents who lean toward the Democratic Party say finding and prosecuting rioters is very important, compared with half of Republicans and Republican leaners.

Similarly, nearly two-thirds of Democrats (65%) say it is likely that the criminal penalties the rioters receive will be less severe than they should be. Republicans are divided: 37% say they are likely to be more severe than they should be, while 26% expect them to be less severe.

Additionally, Democrats express slightly higher confidence in federal law enforcement to find and prosecute those responsible for what happened at the US Capitol in January. Among Democrats who said it was at least somewhat important to find and prosecute those responsible for the Capitol riots, about seven-in-ten Democrats (71%) say they have a great deal (23%) or fair amount (48%) of confidence in federal law enforcement to do so, compared with 66% of Republicans (18% a great deal and 49% a fair amount).

While a plurality of Americans (44%) say the Jan. 6 riot at the US Capitol and its impacts have been getting about the right amount of attention overall, there also are significant differences in these views among Republicans and Democrats.

Many Republicans say the Jan. 6 riots and their aftermath have been getting too much attention (54% say this), which is not a widely shared view among Democrats (8% say too much). By contrast, 40% of Democrats say the riot has been getting too little attention; just 11% of Republicans say the same. About half of Democrats (52%) and a third of Republicans say the riots have gotten about the right amount of attention.

The survey finds that the public expresses more concern about right-wing and left-wing extremism stirring possible violence in the country than either Islamic or Christian extremism. About half of US adults say right-wing extremism (52%) and left-wing extremism (51%) are major problems in the country. Fewer than four-in-ten say violent extremism in the name of Islam (37%) or in the name of Christianity (34%) is a major problem.

Republicans and Democrats are widely divided over which political wing represents the greater threat. About three-quarters of Democrats and Democratic-leaning independents (73%) say right-wing extremism is a major problem, while a similar share of Republicans and Republican leaners (76%) say the same about left-wing extremism. Only about three-in-ten Democrats (31%) say left-wing extremism is a major problem, and 29% of Republicans say this about right-wing extremism.

In addition, Republicans (49%) are more likely than Democrats (28%) to say extremism in the name of Islam is a major problem. The reverse is the case for extremism in the name of Christianity: 48% of Democrats say it is a major problem, versus 16% of Republicans.

Reactions to Aftermath of the Jan. 6 Capitol Riot

Amid continued investigations and congressional hearings into the riots that occurred at the US Capitol on Jan. 6, nearly three-in-ten adults (27%) say there has been too little attention paid to the riots and their impacts. A similar share (28%) says there has been too much attention paid to the events at the Capitol, while a 44% plurality says the riots have received about the right amount of attention.

There are differences in these views by race, partisanship and ideology. Among White adults, 44% say about the right amount of attention has been given to the aftermath of the Capitol riots. Roughly a third (34%) say too much focus has been given to the riots, while a smaller share (21%) says too little attention has been paid.

In contrast, Black adults are significantly more likely to say there has been too little attention paid to the riots and its aftermath: 49% of Black adults say there's been too little, while just 8% say there has been too much focus on the riot.

This racial divide in attitudes is also evident among Democrats and Democratic-leaning adults. While a majority of White Democrats say there has been the right amount of attention paid to the aftermath of the riots (58%), a smaller share of Black Democrats says the same (43%). In fact, more Black Democrats say there has been too little attention given to the riots (50% of Black Democrats vs. 37% of White Democrats).

A majority of Republicans and Republican leaners say there has been too much attention paid to the riot and its impacts (54%). Republicans, unlike Democrats, are divided along ideological lines: 61% of conservative Republicans say the riot and its aftermath have received too much attention, compared with 43% of moderate and liberal Republicans.

Pluralities of Democrats across the ideological spectrum say there has been about the right amount of focus on the Capitol riots and its impacts.

While there is broad consensus across demographic groups that it is at least somewhat important for federal law enforcement to find and prosecute those who broke into the US Capitol on Jan. 6, there is some variation in the degree to which these groups say it is a priority. And while majorities say they have confidence in federal law enforcement agencies to locate and prosecute those involved, relatively small shares express a great deal of confidence that they can do this.

Overall, about eight-in-ten or more adults across demographic groups say it is at least somewhat important for federal law enforcement agencies to seek out those responsible for the Capitol breach (87% overall).

There are racial, ethnic and partisan differences in these views. Black adults are particularly likely to say it is very important for federal law enforcement to penalize those involved (87%); smaller shares of White (66%), Hispanic (69%) and Asian adults (67%) say the same.

There also is a large gap between Republicans and Democrats on the importance of finding and prosecuting those involved in the riots. Just 50% of Republicans say it is very important to find and prosecute those responsible. In contrast, 86% of Democrats say the same.

Among adults who say that finding and prosecuting those who broke into the US Capitol on Jan. 6 is at least somewhat important, 69% also express at least a fair amount of confidence in federal law enforcement to find and prosecute those responsible for the Capitol breach. Relatively small shares of these adults express a great deal of confidence (20% overall).

Among White adults who view prosecution as important, for example, about seven-in-ten express confidence in federal law enforcement agencies to identify and penalize those involved. But while Black adults are among the most likely to say this is important, they are among the least likely to express confidence in federal law enforcement to do this (60%).

This pattern also holds true among Democrats and Democratic leaners who say it is important to prosecute those who broke into the . Nearly eight-in-ten White Democrats (79%) express confidence in federal law enforcement to bring the

Capitol rioters to justice, while just 63% of Black Democrats say the same.

Looking Back at Trump's Impeachment and Acquittal

About a month after former President Donald Trump was acquitted in his second impeachment trial in the Senate, which focused on his conduct leading up to the US Capitol riot, just over half of Americans (52%) say Trump's conduct was wrong, and he should have been convicted by the Senate. About three-in-ten say his conduct was not wrong, and he should not have been impeached, while 15% say his conduct was wrong, but he should not have been convicted by the Senate.

Just as Republicans and Democrats were at odds over whether Trump was responsible for the rioting at the Capitol in early January, partisans view the results of the impeachment trial in very different ways.

Nearly two-thirds of Republicans and GOP leaners (65%) say Trump's conduct was not wrong and he should not have been impeached by the House of Representatives. Nearly a quarter (23%) say his conduct was wrong, but senators should not have voted to convict him. And only 11% of Republicans say that his conduct was wrong, and he should have been convicted by the Senate.

In stark contrast, an overwhelming majority of Democrats and Democratic leaners (87%) say Trump's conduct was wrong, and the Senate should have voted to convict him. Just 9% say his conduct was wrong but he should not have been convicted; another 4% say his conduct was not wrong.

Though Republicans and Democrats express opposing views about several aspects of the rioting that occurred at the US Capitol on Jan. 6, there are stark divisions among Republicans on these issues. Republicans who in January expressed the view that Trump was the rightful winner of the 2020 presidential election are much more likely than those who say Biden won the 2020 election to view the riot as overblown and Trump's impeachment as unjustified.

In January 2021, when asked which candidate won the 2020 presidential election, 64% of Republicans and Republican leaners said that Trump definitely (33%) or probably (31%) received the most votes cast by eligible voters in enough states to win the presidential election. Only about a third (34%) said correctly that Biden was the rightful winner.

Republicans who said Trump definitely or probably won the election earlier this year are nearly twice as likely as Republicans who said Biden definitely or probably won to now say the riots at the Capitol have received too much attention (66% of Republicans who say Trump won vs. 35% of Republicans who say Biden won). Similarly, while 62% of Republicans who said Biden won now say that it is very important that federal law enforcement agencies find and prosecute those who broke into the US Capitol on Jan. 6, fewer than half of Republicans who said Trump won now say prosecution is very important.

This pattern is also evident in views of the punishments that rioters are likely to receive. Republicans who said Biden won in the prior survey are now significantly less likely than Republicans who said Trump won to think the criminal penalties that rioters will receive are likely to be more severe than they should be (27% vs. 45%, respectively).

One of the largest gaps that divides Republicans who said Trump won and Republicans who said Biden won is on views of Trump's impeachment as a result of his conduct leading up to events on Jan. 6: Fully 82% of Republicans who said Trump won the election say his conduct was not wrong, and that the House should not have voted to impeach him. This compares with just 26% of Republicans who said Biden won the 2020 election.

Views of Violent Extremism

When it comes to the possibility of violent extremism in the country, Americans are more likely to say political extremism

Should Those Who Stormed the Capitol Be Harshly Punished?

represents a greater problem than other forms of extremism inspired by religion.

About half of the public says right-wing extremism is a major problem (52%), another third say it is a minor problem and 12% say it is not a problem. The public's overall views of left-wing extremism are similar: 51% say it is a major problem, 34% say minor problem and 13% say not a problem.

The shares saying extremism inspired by Islam or Christianity are major problems are far lower. Slightly fewer than four-in-ten adults (37%) say extremism inspired by Islam is a major problem, while 44% say it is a minor problem and 16% say it is not a problem. About a third of Americans (34%) say extremism in the name of Christianity is a major problem, with 35% saying it is a minor problem and 29% say it is not a problem.

While far more Republicans view left-wing extremism as a major problem than right-wing extremism—and the opposite is true among Democrats—large majorities in both parties say right-wing and left-wing extremism are major or minor problems.

Among Republicans and Republican-leaning independents, only about three-in-ten (29%) say violent right-wing extremism is a major problem for the country, but about half (49%) say it is a minor problem. Just two-in-ten say it is not a problem.

Views among Democrats and Democratic leaners of left-wing extremism follow a similar pattern: About three-in-ten (31%) say left-wing extremist violence is a major problem, about half say it is a minor problem (48%) and just 19% say it is not a problem.

Both Republicans and Democrats broadly acknowledge that violent extremism inspired by Islam is at least a minor problem in the country (88% of Republicans and 78% of Democrats say this). However, Republicans are more likely than Democrats to view Islamic extremism as a major problem (49% of Republicans vs. 28% of Democrats).

They also differ on whether extremism inspired by Christianity is a problem for the country: 83% of Democrats say Christian extremism is at least a minor problem (including 48% saying it is a major problem), yet only about half of Republicans (51%) say it is at least a minor problem (with just 16% saying major problem). Nearly half of Republicans (47%) say extremism in the name of Christianity is not a problem in the country today.

In both parties, there are ideological differences in attitudes about the threat posed by violent extremism. For example, a larger share of liberal Democrats (83%) than conservative and moderate Democrats (66%) say right-wing extremism is a major problem. By contrast, conservative Republicans are more likely than moderate and liberal Republicans to say that left-wing extremism is a major problem.

Moderates and liberals in the GOP also are more likely than conservative Republicans to see right-wing extremism (39% to 23%) as a major problem. And conservative and moderate Democrats similarly diverge from liberals in their party in views of left-wing extremism (41% of conservative and moderate Democrats say major problem vs. 18% of liberals).

There are similar patterns across ideological groups in their views of religious extremism—though the differences are generally smaller. Fewer moderate and liberal Republicans than conservative Republicans say extremism in the name of Islam is a major problem (42% vs. 53%) and more say extremism inspired by Christianity is a major problem (23% vs. 12%). The patterns are similar but reversed among Democrats: Fewer conservative and moderate Democrats than liberal Democrats say Christian extremists are a major problem (38% vs. 59%), but more moderate and liberal Democrats say Islamic extremists are a major problem (34% vs. 21%).

Knowledge of QAnon and Views of Its Supporters

A majority of Americans (61%) report knowing at least something about the QAnon conspiracy theories, while about four-in-ten

Should Those Who Stormed the Capitol Be Harshly Punished?

(39%) say they know "nothing at all" about them. Few US adults say they know "a lot" (3%), while 29% say they know "some" and the same share say they know "not much."

Democrats and independents who lean toward the Democratic Party (68%) are more likely than Republicans and Republican leaners (54%) to say they know something about the QAnon conspiracy theories. Nearly half of Republicans (45%) say they know nothing at all about them; about three-in-ten Democrats (31%) say the same.

Liberal Democrats report the highest levels of knowledge about QAnon. Half of liberal Democrats know a lot (7%) or some (44%) about it, and another 28% say they know not much. The next most knowledgeable groups are conservative and moderate Democrats (61% know something, including 32% who know some or a lot) and conservative Republicans (60% know something, including 25% some or a lot). The least knowledgeable partisans are Republicans with moderate or liberal political views—among this group, a majority say they know nothing at all about these conspiracy theories (54%) and fewer than a quarter know a lot or some (22%).

Few Americans who know at least something about QAnon have favorable views of people who support the conspiracy theories. Just 13% of those who know about QAnon have favorable views of its supporters, while 84% have unfavorable views (including 60% whose views are very unfavorable).

Those who say their views of QAnon supporters are favorable are concentrated among Republicans and Republican-leaning independents. About a quarter of Republicans who know about QAnon say they view its supporters favorably (24%)—though just 5% say their views are very favorable, compared with 19% who say somewhat favorable. Fewer than one-in-ten Democrats and Democratic leaners (6%) have favorable views of QAnon supporters.

Most Republicans and Democrats say they view people who support these conspiracy theories unfavorably, though

Democrats are harsher in their judgments. Fully 82% of Democrats who know about QAnon say they have very unfavorable views of supporters, versus 28% Republicans who share this view. About four-in-ten Republicans who know about QAnon (42%) have somewhat unfavorable views of QAnon supporters; 12% of Democrats say the same.

The Capitol Was Invaded Because of a Failure to Punish Those Who Had Attacked State Capitols

Jeremy Kohler

Jeremy Kohler is a reporter covering issues in the Midwest. He formerly worked as an investigative reporter at the St. Louis Post-Dispatch, *where he produced projects that exposed fraud and abuse in policing, prisons, pension systems, hospitals, and courts.*

The gallery in the Idaho House was restricted to limited seating on the first day of a special session in late August. Lawmakers wanted space to socially distance as they considered issues related to the pandemic and the November election.

But maskless protesters shoved their way past Idaho State Police troopers and security guards, broke through a glass door and demanded entry. They were confronted by House Speaker Scott Bedke, a Republican. He decided to let them in and fill the gallery.

"You guys are going to police yourselves up there, and you're going to act like good citizens," he told the invaders, according to a YouTube video of the incident.

"I just thought that, on balance, it would be better to let them go in and defuse it … rather than risk anyone getting hurt or risk tearing up anything else," Bedke said of the protesters in an interview last week. He said he talked to cooler heads in the crowd "who saw that it was a situation that had gotten out of control, and I think on some level they were very apologetic."

That late-summer showdown inside the Statehouse in Boise on Aug. 24 showed supporters of President Donald Trump how they could storm into a seat of government to intimidate lawmakers

"'Sense of Entitlement': Rioters Faced Few Consequences Invading State Capitols. No Wonder They Turned to the US Capitol Next," by Jeremy Kohler, Propublica, January 19, 2021. Reprinted by permission.

with few if any repercussions. The state police would say later that they could not have arrested people without escalating the potential for violence and that they were investigating whether crimes were committed. No charges have been filed. The next day, anti-government activist Ammon Bundy and two others were arrested when they refused to leave an auditorium in the Statehouse and another man was arrested when he refused to leave a press area.

In a year in which state governments around the country have become flashpoints for conservative anger about the coronavirus lockdown and Trump's electoral defeat, it was right-wing activists—some of them armed, nearly all of them white—who forced their way into state capitols in Idaho, Michigan and Oregon. Each instance was an opportunity for local and national law enforcement officials to school themselves in ways to prevent angry mobs from threatening the nation's lawmakers.

But it was Trump supporters who did the learning. That it was possible—even easy—to breach the seats of government to intimidate lawmakers. That police would not meet them with the same level of force they deployed against Black Lives Matter protesters. That they could find sympathizers on the inside who might help them.

And they learned that criminal charges, as well as efforts to make the buildings more secure, were unlikely to follow their incursions. In the three cases, police made only a handful of arrests.

The failure to stop state capitol invasions is especially chilling after the attack on the US Capitol last week, which left five dead, including a police officer, as lawmakers met to certify the election of President-elect Joe Biden.

Experts and elected officials said the lack of action by lawmakers and police created an environment that encouraged political violence. The FBI has warned of armed protests occurring in all 50 state capitols in the run-up to the inauguration on Wednesday. Authorities in both Washington and state capitols have dramatically strengthened security.

"Eventually, you get to the point of entitlement where you can get away with anything and there will never be any accountability," the Idaho House minority leader, Ilana Rubel, a Democrat, said. "I don't know that (Bedke) was wrong under the circumstances, but it adds up to creating a sense of entitlement."

Bedke said he saw no correlation between the events in Boise and Washington. But domestic terror experts said in interviews that the statehouse invasions likely created a sense of impunity among right-wing activists. The feeling grew throughout the year as Trump praised gun-carrying activists at state capitols as "very good people" and emboldened the insurrectionists in Washington.

Amy Cooter, a Vanderbilt University sociologist and expert in the militia movement, said the US Capitol attack may have been less likely to occur if the violence in state capitols had been met with harsher punishment.

What's more, she said that authorities who failed to take action against protesters earlier may find it difficult to do so now.

While many Trump supporters already see their First Amendment rights as being under attack, they may see efforts to block them from state capitols as an attack on their Second Amendment rights, she said, further legitimizing their need to stand up to what they perceive as tyranny.

When officials acquiesce to demands, "it typically makes these folks feel like those are 'constitutional' officials who support their general aims, which can then embolden them against officials they believe to be the opposite, that is, officials they believe to be betraying their oaths to the people," Cooter said.

If extremist groups "believe they have been given allowances in the past and are not moving forward, this can further reinforce that notion of officials who are derelict in their duty, officials who should be removed and, depending on what group we're talking about, possibly officials who should be confronted with force."

Days after Trump tweeted "LIBERATE MICHIGAN," protesters taking part in an "American Patriot Rally" outside the Michigan Capitol in Lansing on April 30 swarmed into the building demanding an end to the stay-at-home order put in place by Gov. Gretchen Whitmer to combat the COVID-19 pandemic.

The group, which numbered in the hundreds, included several heavily armed men. Few wore face coverings or observed social distancing. A line of state police troopers and other Capitol employees held the mob back from entering the House floor.

"We had hundreds of individuals storm our Capitol building," state Rep. Sarah Anthony said in an interview. "No, lives were not lost, blood was not shed, property was not damaged, but I think they saw how easy it was to get into our building and they could get away with that type of behavior and there would be little to no consequences."

Some armed invaders entered the Senate gallery. While none of the protesters faced charges, two of the men seen in a photo posted by state Sen. Dayna Polehanki looking down on lawmakers would be among the 14 people charged months later in a plot to kidnap Whitmer and bomb the state Capitol.

"It made national and international news, what happened in our Capitol," Polehanki said in an interview. "People saw that, and it's no coincidence that the storming of the US Capitol on Jan. 6 had the same feel."

Polehanki, a Democrat from Livonia, asked the state's Republican-majority Senate to support a resolution banning firearms in the Capitol. But it wasn't until Jan. 11, five days after the US Capitol insurrection, that the Michigan Capitol Commission voted to ban the open carry of guns inside the building. Open carry is still allowed outside the building, and people who have concealed pistol licenses can still carry concealed weapons inside.

Michigan Attorney General Dana Nessel tweeted that visitors should stay away from the state Capitol because it is "not safe." Some legislators have begun wearing bulletproof vests.

The memories of the April 30 invasion still haunt Anthony, a Democrat from Lansing. "The level of anxiety and fear that was intended to be imposed upon those of us in the building will probably stay with me for the rest of my life."

As the legislators convened to vote, Anthony said she sat next to state Rep. Brenda Carter, D-Pontiac, another Black woman who was afraid of being targeted by the invaders. "We look like Democrats, so I think when you have individuals who are not only carrying large firearms but also carrying Confederate flags and nooses and swastikas, those have specific messages targeted to Black and brown communities."

Days later, she arrived at the Capitol building with an escort from five armed constituents.

An angry mob didn't need to break down a door to enter the Oregon Statehouse in Salem to disrupt a one-day special session on Dec. 21. A surveillance video released two days after the US Capitol insurrection revealed that Republican state Rep. Mike Nearman, of Independence, opened a locked side door to let in some violent protesters.

The building, normally open to the public, had been closed since mid-March because of health concerns. But several dozen demonstrators gathered outside in a "flash mob" organized by the far-right group Patriot Prayer, which has been tied to protests in Portland. Dozens of rioters streamed into the building and attacked police officers.

One of the Patriot Prayer supporters who carried an AR-15 rifle into the Statehouse was charged with pepper-spraying six police officers. Five other protesters were also taken into custody.

Nearman would later issue a statement defending his action by noting the state Constitution mandates open public legislative proceedings. He was removed from legislative committees and billed for damages caused by the rioters. House Speaker Tina Kotek, D-Portland, called on him to resign. Nearman and Kotek did not respond to requests for comment.

Nearman's conduct had parallels to concerns among some in Congress that perpetrators of the US Capitol attack had help from police or even lawmakers. Rep. Mikie Sherrill, D-N.J., said she witnessed lawmakers giving "reconnaissance" tours the day before the Capitol attack.

"They couldn't have done what they are doing without some notion of impunity around it," said Lawrence Rosenthal, chair and lead researcher of the Center for Right-Wing Studies at the University of California-Berkeley. He said militants cling to a fantasy that if a civil war were to break out, what some extremists call a boogaloo, police and the military would join their side. Those notions may have been corroborated at the state capitols, Rosenthal said. "The type of wink-wink quality that these guys experienced."

At least three men involved in the effort to invade the Oregon Statehouse appeared to have joined the insurrection at the U.S Capitol, according to Oregon Public Broadcasting.

One of them, Tim Davis, 59, of Springfield, Oregon, told ProPublica he "couldn't comment" about whether the riot in Salem inspired him to travel to the nation's capital. He insisted he did not join those who entered the US Capitol building or break any laws.

"The president asked people to come, and I felt it was my constitutional duty to go," he said.

Congress Must Defend the Constitution

Niskanen Center

The Niskanen Center is a nonpartisan think tank that works to promote an open society.

Donald Trump was rightly impeached for his role in the appalling events of January 6, 2021. Now, the Senate must vote to convict and disqualify Trump from any future federal office without delay.

However, Trump is not solely responsible for the treacherous assault on the Capitol. Members of Congress who vouched for the president's lies about election fraud must also be sanctioned for their role. And those who went even further, planning and participating in the protest that birthed the mob, should be removed from office.

Unlike in the president's case, there must be no rush to justice. Truth is paramount. The culpability of Congress members must be established with scrupulous objectivity and care, without fear or favor. Investigations into various aspects of the insurrection by the relevant House and Senate committees are critically necessary. However, because perceptions of partisan opportunism must be avoided at all costs, the work of telling the whole story, and assigning responsibility to members of Congress for the parts they played in it, is best carried out by a non-partisan, independent commission similar to the 9/11 commission. That's why Congress should work across the aisle to create and empower such a commission, and commit to carrying out its recommendations.

A brief review of the facts so far shows that the case for the president's immediate conviction and removal, and the creation of an independent commission, could hardly be stronger.

On January 6, 2021, a seditious mob incited by President Trump descended upon the Capitol with the express purpose of menacing

---

"Congress Must Defend the Constitution: Convict, Disqualify, Investigate and Sanction," Niskanen Center, January 19, 2021, https://www.niskanencenter.org/congress-must-defend-the-constitution-convict-disqualify-investigate-and-sanction/. Licensed under CC BY 4.0 International.

the ongoing certification of the 2020 election. A portion of the larger group smashed and battered its way into the Capitol, disrupting Congress as it tallied the states' electoral votes.

The swarm of Trump loyalists, animated by the president's outrageous lies about election fraud, swiftly overwhelmed meager lines of Capitol Police. One officer was killed in the siege. Another was dragged into the mob and brutally beaten with boots, fists, and a flagpole bearing the Stars and Stripes. The mob routed both houses of Congress from their chambers. Members of the House and Senate, fearing for their lives, were forced into hiding. Repeated requests for federal backup were ignored, denied, and then only belatedly fulfilled by Trump administration officials, leaving Congress stranded for hours in grave danger. Rioters set up a gallows outside the Capitol and howled for the lynching of Vice President Mike Pence—an act that some of the rioters seem to have entered the Capitol with grave intent to carry out. Trump loyalists bristling with military gear roamed the halls and chambers of Congress seeking to abduct and kill elected representatives of the American people.

If not for the alacrity and courage of Capitol Police officers who delayed the mob and led members of Congress out of harm's way, the worst among the insurrectionists might have succeeded in carrying out horrific acts of political terror. The discovery of bombs and other caches of weapons near the Capitol—together with eyewitness reports, social media chatter, and the invaders' own self-recorded footage—has made it chillingly clear that the sack of the Capitol, as terrifying as it was, might have become a blood-soaked massacre.

Donald Trump was impeached last week by the House of Representatives for "incitement of insurrection." There can be no doubt that this was justified. From the moment it became clear he would lose the election, Donald Trump worked tirelessly to discredit the result and disrupt the transfer of power to president-elect Joseph Biden. The deadly riot that ensued from his speech at the "Stop the Steal" rally was the logical culmination of this effort to undermine the democratic process. For the last two months, the president has inflamed his supporters with the groundless lie that the election was stolen. With the help of allied politicians and media outlets eager to repeat and amplify his lies, the president was able to work his devoted base into a lather of incendiary indignation. On January 6, he charged them up and set them loose on Congress.

The ten House Republicans who voted for impeachment— Liz Cheney, Tom Rice, Dan Newhouse, Adam Kinzinger, Anthony Gonzalez, Fred Upton, Jaime Herrera Beutler, Peter Meijer, John Katko, and David Valadao — deserve honor and gratitude for rising to the defense of country and Constitution in the face of violent threats and intense partisan pressure. Their valor and integrity fatally undermines the dangerous claim that Trump's second impeachment was nothing more than a vindictive act of partisan hostility.

Now that he has been impeached (again), Donald Trump must be convicted by the Senate, and permanently barred from federal office. Every hour he has remained in office, steadfast in the lies that fed the mob's fury, the civil peace and the stability of our rattled Republic has been at risk. Allowing a president to complete his term after fomenting a violent assault on Congress is bad enough. Refusing to convict, or avoiding a Senate trial altogether, would render the Constitution's mechanisms of executive accountability meaningless, setting a dangerous precedent that could invite the collapse of our constitutional order.

The peaceful transfer of power, and the losing party's assent to the legitimacy of the electoral process, are essential to preserving American democracy. Trump trampled over that sacred principle— sinned unforgivably against the stability of republican self-rule. The Senate must now act in the interests of all Americans to lessen the likelihood that any future chief executive will be tempted to follow Trump's demagogic example.

There is too much at stake to further delay mounting a trial, or to draw it out for days or weeks past Biden's inauguration. There is no need for a lengthy Senate trial because the facts that justify impeachment and removal are not obscure. The only real questions are the meanings that Senators will attach to those facts and the considerations, both moral and prudential, that will shape their final decision.

The Senate must consider, above all, whether the threat of violence and mob rule will be allowed to loom over the deliberations of the first branch of government. Trump sent his mob to the Capitol to make that threat vivid in the minds of legislators. If such a sensational act of violent intimidation is not repudiated and punished in the strongest possible terms, the events of January 6 are destined to presage a plague of political violence—one that will spread to every state Capitol in this country.

The choice now is to stand up to the mob and the demagogues who have inflamed them or accept a politics that operates in the shadow of violence for years to come. Republicans, in particular, must bear in mind that the mob descended on the Capitol to intimidate them. The noose was meant for Mike Pence, not Nancy Pelosi. Trump loyalists, emboldened by the riot, are already threatening Republican legislators to scare them into falling in line. Some have confessed to the fear that voting against Trump will be met with violent reprisal. Therefore, decent Republicans must consider whether they wish to submit to the rule of their party's most violent faction. If they fail to summon the courage to bring the hammer down on Trump, they may very well lose control of their party to the lawless extremism that he has cultivated within its ranks.

Impeachment and conviction of the president do not exhaust the necessary measures in the aftermath of January 6. Trump must also be held legally accountable for any crimes he may have committed, which will be doubly necessary should the Senate again fail in its duty.

Blame for the insurrectionary riots cannot be laid entirely at Donald Trump's feet. Many Congress members actively encouraged Americans to believe that the election was tainted by fraud, that Biden may not have been legitimately elected, and that our democracy could be irreparably harmed should he be allowed to take office. They should be held responsible for the dire consequences of propagating these lies. The worst offenders may merit official censure or worse.

Most deserve to be abandoned by donors, saddled with strong primary challengers, and punished by voters at the ballot box.

It appears that some Republican members did more than amplify destabilizing falsehoods. Some may have actively planned to bring a mob to the Capitol steps with the intent of influencing the electoral count. If that is the case, they should be removed from Congress and face criminal prosecution.

However, it is essential that any such sanctions imposed on Congress members be grounded in a scrupulous, comprehensive accounting of the factors that contributed to the siege. This disaster was caused by the opportunistic deployment of lies for political gain. If we are to have any hope of restoring stable, functional, constitutional government, the process by which we investigate these events and mete out justice must be a model of careful, proper procedure.

Amy Zegart and Herbert Lin of Stanford University have developed a careful proposal for a commission on January 6, based on an extensive assessment of past commissions (including the 9/11 commission). Congress should expeditiously create such a commission and commit across the aisle to follow its findings, wherever they may lead.

Donald Trump authored this dark, destabilizing, deadly chapter in our nation's history with antagonism toward justice and contempt for the truth. Unless we hasten to rebalance the scales of justice, restore the supremacy of fact, and re-commit to a common reality and common good, Donald Trump's reprehensible legacy will linger like a toxic fog and continue to poison our public life long after he has gone.

Restraint Must Be Used When Considering Harsh Punishments for the Capitol Rioters

Eric Westervelt

Eric Westervelt is a San Francisco-based correspondent for National Public Radio's national desk. He has reported on major events for the network, from wars and revolutions in the Middle East and North Africa to historic wildfires and terrorist attacks in the United States.

Legal scholars and prosecutors are debating whether federal charges of seditious conspiracy should be used against some of the pro-Trump rioters that stormed the US Capitol building last week.

RACHEL MARTIN, HOST:
The impeachment resolution against President Trump charges him with, quote, inciting violence against the government of the United States. A House vote on that article could come as soon as tomorrow. As for the pro-Trump rioters who attacked the US Capitol, they face a range of charges. Should something called seditious conspiracy be among them? NPR's Eric Westervelt is with us now. Good morning, Eric.

ERIC WESTERVELT, BYLINE: Good morning.

MARTIN: There's this big toolbox of federal charges that could be used in this situation. Sedition is one of the most serious. Federal code, Section 2384 defines it as a conspiracy to, quote, "overthrow, put down or destroy the government by force." What else should we know about this charge?

©2021 National Public Radio, Inc. NPR news report titled "Should Capitol Rioters Be Charged With Seditious Conspiracy?" was originally broadcast on NPR's Morning Edition on January 12, 2021, and is used with the permission of NPR. Any unauthorized duplication is strictly prohibited.

WESTERVELT: Well, beyond that language about a plot to overthrow the government, the code says, you know, it's seditious conspiracy if two or more persons use force to, quote, "prevent, hinder or delay the execution of any law of the US or by force, seize, take or possess any property of the US" And rioters certainly used force to try to prevent, hinder or delay Congress from formalizing the Electoral College vote for Joe Biden as president. I mean, they were able to delay the Congress for hours - so clearly an attempt to halt what in saner times was seen as something of a formality, but is still, perhaps, the most important function Congress carries out.

MARTIN: Right. So do legal experts think the government would have a strong case if they brought sedition charges?

WESTERVELT: They do. But it's tough. And bigger questions are, you know, why go down that path? What are prosecutors really trying to achieve when there's other charges? I spoke with retired Brigadier General Michael McDaniel. He now teaches constitutional law at Western Michigan University.

MICHAEL MCDANIEL: I think that there has to be successful criminal prosecutions of these individuals that were involved in seditious conspiracy. Anybody who broke in with the intent to stop the vote, that's sedition. That is textbook sedition.

WESTERVELT: Seditious conspiracy charges have been used a handful of times in modern America with very mixed success. The statute worked against Islamist terrorists, including the sheikh who masterminded the 1993 World Trade Center bombing. But its most recent use in 2010 against the far-right Hutaree militia in Michigan did not go well. Members of the self-described Christian militia were accused of plotting to kill a police officer and bomb his funeral in hopes of sparking an anti-government uprising. A judge dismissed the sedition charges, ruling the government failed to prove the group planned to carry out specific attacks. Three members were convicted of lesser weapons charges and sentenced to time served. Andy Arena led that investigation when he was special agent in charge of the FBI's Detroit division. Today, some Capitol rioters, he says, may well meet the terms of the sedition statute. But he cautions it's a pretty high bar.

ANDREW ARENA: It's hard to prove. I'm not saying they can't do it here. I'm not saying they shouldn't charge it. It's just you've got to make sure you've got all your ducks in a row because it's tough.

WESTERVELT: Asked if he's considering sedition charges, the federal prosecutor in charge, acting US attorney for the District of Columbia Michael Sherwin, tells NPR, yes. All charges are on the table as long as the evidence fits the criminal charge. And evidence of equipment and even loose organization may help show intent. US Attorney Sherwin tells NPR that while it's not clear there was any overall command and control by rioters, there's certainly evidence of coordination.

MICHAEL SHERWIN: They look paramilitary almost, right? The uniform, you've got communication, those show indications of affiliation and a command and control. So I believe we are going to find those hallmarks. I can't say when. I think it could be weeks, if not months.

WESTERVELT: Those hallmarks are likely to prove key in any potential sedition case, says former FBI agent Arena, now director of the Detroit Crime Commission and a law professor. He says the fact that many rioters boasted on social media about their intent to stop the Electoral College count and set up a makeshift gallows and showed off gear could make any sedition case a little easier.
ARENA: These weren't the brightest guys, you know? I mean (laughter), you see it. I mean, guys are showing up there with rappelling equipment, zip ties. I mean, they're looking to handcuff people. I mean, why else are you doing that, right? So they weren't

going there to exercise their First Amendment free speech, to protest. They were going there to get it on.

WESTERVELT: And some legal experts say if sedition is not among those charges, it risks further normalizing the kind of political violence we've seen in the Trump era from Charlottesville to the Capitol. Again, law professor Michael McDaniel at western Michigan.

MCDANIEL: This dark barrel of political violence has been opened. And once opened, you can't put the lid back on it easily. Any sort of symbolic or real gathering of government officials is going to be subjected to the possibility of political violence from these groups.

WESTERVELT: But others strongly caution against going down sedition road.

SHIRIN SINNAR: You know, I don't disagree that they should be prosecuted. But the most important efforts are political and not simply aggressively deploying criminal law.

WESTERVELT: Shirin Sinnar is a professor at Stanford Law School. She warns that seditious conspiracy charges could easily boomerang in the years ahead and end up being used to stifle dissent, especially by people of color and other historically marginalized groups.

SINNAR: We've got a long history of using sedition laws to suppress dissent. And although that's not what those who were invading the Capitol were doing—they were engaged in action, not just speech - we still need to be careful about expanding a framework that's been so connected to the suppression of ideas.

WESTERVELT: Following shocking crime, Sinnar says, America too often goes after low-hanging fruit and turns its gaze away from the much more powerful systems that enabled them. Eric Westervelt, NPR News.

The Capitol Rioters Believe That Trump Owed Them Pardons
Kevin Rector and Chris Megarian

Kevin Rector is a reporter for the Los Angeles Times, *where he covers the Los Angeles Police Department. Chris Megerian covers the White House from the* Los Angeles Times' *DC bureau.*

They launched their assault on the US Capitol with impunity, livestreaming their crimes and posing for photos as they breached the building's perimeter and threatened the democratic process. Now members of the pro-Trump mob are arguing they shouldn't be held to account.

Speaking through defense lawyers or in interviews, the alleged rioters argued they did nothing illegal. They couldn't have been trespassing, they say, because they entered the Capitol at the "invitation" of President Trump, following his direct orders. Capitol police also held the doors open for them, they assert, basically ushering them into the building's hallowed halls. Even so, knowing that time is running out on Trump's presidency, they are also making a last-minute case for clemency to avert prosecution, appealing to the man who allegedly incited them to act.

"I would like a pardon from the president of the United States," said Jenna Ryan, a Texas real estate agent charged in the storming of the Capitol, in an interview with CBS News late last week. "I think that we all deserve a pardon. I'm facing a prison sentence. I think that I do not deserve that."

Adam Newbold, a retired US Navy SEAL, told ABC News that he was seeking "clemency" after posting a Facebook video boasting about "breaching the Capitol," which brought FBI agents to his door for an interview.

"Alleged Capitol Rioters Argue Trump Invited Them in, and Now They Want Pardons," by Kevin Rector and Chris Megarian, *LA Times*, January 19, 2021. Reprinted by permission.

"I would like to express to you just a cry for clemency, as you understand that my life now has been absolutely turned upside-down," Newbold said.

An attorney for Jacob Chansley—the man who entered the Capitol wearing horns and carrying a spear—said on CNN that his client also deserved a pardon, as he was only in the Capitol because he had "hitched his wagon" to Trump and felt he was answering a "call" from the president to go there.

"The words and invitation of a president are supposed to mean something," said the attorney, Albert Watkins.

Trump had called his supporters to the National Mall on Jan. 6 for what he said would be a "wild" protest, a continuation of his months-long falsehood-filled campaign to overturn an election he lost. He then egged them on during a rally speech to head to the Capitol as Congress was counting electoral votes for Biden. His actions led House Democrats, joined by 10 Republicans, to impeach Trump last week, making him the first president to twice face that sanction. Lawmakers said he incited the mob attack, setting up a Senate trial that will take place when Biden is president. Biden is set to be sworn in on Wednesday.

Although the prosecutions are in their early stages, scholars and legal experts say the alleged rioters' early pronouncements—that their fealty to Trump should get them leniency in return—reflect a deeply rooted sense of entitlement among many supporters of Trump, who for years has projected a swaggering disregard for his own legal troubles and a penchant for pardoning his confidants.

"Impunity is in some ways kind of the defining feature of Trump as a public personality and of the Trump presidency. He has taken impunity to an art form," said Brian DeLay, an associate professor of history at UC Berkeley.

In both his impeachments, in the special counsel probe into Russia's interference in the 2016 campaign, and in case after case in which associates have been charged and convicted of crimes, Trump has telegraphed to his supporters that he—and they—

are beyond reproach, castigating investigations as witch hunts or hoaxes.

"Impunity is something that has been baked into Trumpism from the beginning," DeLay said, "and so it's not surprising to me now that the people who consider themselves his followers are saying, I think in a pretty authentic way, 'Surely you're going to get us out of this. You asked us to do it, we did it, and impunity is how things work.'"

The alleged rioters' hope may not be entirely misplaced.

Trump has used his clemency power almost exclusively as a political tool to reward supporters. His first pardon went to Joe Arpaio, the former sheriff of Arizona's Maricopa County, who was held in contempt of court for refusing to stop racially profiling Latinos. The following year, at the urging of Kim Kardashian, he commuted the sentence of Alice Johnson, who was serving a life term for a nonviolent drug offense. He later pardoned Johnson after she supported his reelection campaign.

The president has also almost completely undone the sentences handed down during the Russia investigation, pardoning nearly every former advisor who was convicted or pleaded guilty, including former national security advisor Michael Flynn, former campaign Chairman Paul Manafort and longtime political advisor Roger Stone.

Overt appeals for clemency have been welcomed by Trump. He's come to the aid of accused and convicted war criminals after their supporters or lawyers have made pleas for help on Fox News.

It's unclear if Trump is considering pardoning any of those who breached the Capitol's security. The Department of Justice said in a statement that its Office of the Pardon Attorney "is not involved in any efforts to pardon individuals or groups involved with the heinous acts that took place this week in and around the US Capitol," although the president has typically circumvented the normal procedure for weighing clemency.

Steven Levin, a former federal prosecutor and military judge who is now a criminal defense lawyer, says he thinks it is unlikely

Should Those Who Stormed the Capitol Be Harshly Punished?

Trump will pardon the rioters. Doing so, he said, "would be further evidence that they were doing his bidding."

Despite their protestations that the president urged them on, the defendants are also likely to fail in court because an invitation to commit a crime is not an excuse to do it, Levin said.

To make his point, Levin—who is not representing anyone accused in the riot—compared the siege of the Capitol to a bank robbery.

"You can't really make the argument that, 'Hey look, the bank president invited me in with my friends so we could take money from the vault.' That doesn't make it legal," Levin said. "No jury is going to find that argument sympathetic or, frankly, even reasonable."

Some of the accused also have claimed that they didn't break into the Capitol but were let in by police.

Watkins, the attorney for the spear-wielding Chansley, argued on CNN that Chansley "did not break into" the building but "had the doors to the Capitol held for him by Capitol Police."

Thomas Robertson, a Virginia police officer, made a similar assertion to investigators in trying to explain why he entered the building, according to court papers.

Levin said such arguments were almost certain to fail. Police officers who feared for their own safety and were overwhelmed by the sheer size of the advancing crowd had legitimate reasons for not attempting to halt the intruders.

Levin said defendants—particularly those charged with unlawful entry, especially those who know images of them in the building are out there—would "be wise to negotiate a deal" as soon as possible.

Why Should the Rioters Be Punished and Not Their Enablers?

Julie Erfle

Julie Erfle launched the political blog Politics Uncuffed in 2011 and began working as a communications director and consultant on candidate and initiative campaigns. She is the former executive director of Progress Now Arizona, a progressive communications and advocacy nonprofit and a fellow with the Flinn-Brown Arizona Center for Civic Leadership and Leading for Change.

I have no empathy for the insurrectionists who tore through the Capitol, intent on overturning the results of our election and installing Donald Trump as some sort of king.

Many will be fired from their jobs and end up in prison, which is exactly what they deserve.

Nor do I believe that those involved in securing the Capitol who ignored warnings and put frontline officers in peril or those officers who posed for selfies or helped insurrectionists trample through the halls of Congress should avoid punishment.

But what about those who encouraged the actions of the insurrectionists—the elected officials, media outlets and corporate executives who profited from years of chaos and division? Will they be allowed to simply condemn the violence, then move on as if they couldn't have predicted this outcome, as if they played no role in this shameful moment in our history?

For the past several years, many of us have reacted with shock and anger as Donald Trump broke one norm after another. We couldn't understand how so many people, most especially our elected officials, could choose to ignore the president's actions or worse yet, condone and embolden his disgraceful behavior.

"The Rioters and Capitol Police Will Be Punished, but Not the Instigators and Enablers? How Is that Fair?" by Julie Erfle, AZMirror, January 12, 2021. https://www.azmirror.com/2021/01/12/the-rioters-and-capitol-police-will-be-punished-but-not-the-instigators-and-enablers-how-is-that-fair/. Reprinted by permission.

Don't take him so seriously, the enablers told us, when Trump celebrated violence against the media and openly courted white supremacists and alt-right organizations.

Look at how he's triggering the libs, they laughed when we took offense to him calling women dogs (among other things) and African nations shithole countries and telling sitting members of Congress to go back where they came from.

They shrugged off his Muslim travel ban, his "perfect call" with the Ukrainian president, and his attacks on federal judges and military families and attempted to justify and deflect blame when the children of migrants were taken from their parents and placed in cold, filthy cages fit for wild animals or serial killers, not toddlers in need of diaper changes and human touch.

And all of Trump's lies? Totally worth it because he appointed conservative judges and cut taxes for wealthy Americans and corporations.

It's only now—after a failed coup that sought to topple our democracy—that these same politicians and corporations and media outlets are finally alarmed enough to stop parroting and excusing Donald Trump.

But that's not enough.

Some have recommended that Congress create an independent commission, much like the 9-11 Commission, to examine how we came to the events of January 6 and how we could prevent our nation from ever traveling down that same path.

I support this, though I believe many of us already understand how this happened. The question is, can we prevent it from happening again?

I believe we can, but not if our focus remains solely on security lapses and rioters. We must also hold the instigators and the enablers to account.

In Arizona, the seditious instigators have been obvious. They include GOP Chair Kelli Ward, US Reps. Paul Gosar and Andy Biggs, state Rep. Mark Finchem and state senators Wendy Rogers and Kelly Townsend (among others).

This group of seditionists helped forward election conspiracies and lies in an attempt to disenfranchise millions of voters and overturn the election. Some even used not-so-coded language to hint at the possibility of using force. They haven't backed down from their baseless claims, even after last week's attempted coup, showing their allegiance is not to the country and our Constitution, but to Donald Trump. They should be removed from office.

But what about the enablers? State politicians such as Gov. Doug Ducey and Attorney General Mark Brnovich? Like so many elected Republicans, they courted and appeased Trump.

Some have suggested they're off the hook. After all, Ducey certified Arizona's election results, and Brnovich dropped his investigation into #sharpiegate when it became obvious it was nothing but an unfounded conspiracy.

But is doing what is legally required by law—basically, the bare minimum—really a profile in courage? Shouldn't the governor and AG still provide a mea culpa for their love fest with a dangerous, dictator wannabe?

Ducey and allies have condemned the violence, but they've yet to condemn Donald Trump or take any responsibility whatsoever for their role in enabling dangerous rhetoric and the shattering of norms that offered Trump's lies legitimacy and led to last week's insurrection.

Instead, Republican enablers are using a new buzzword to talk about what comes next: unity.

We can hold the insurrectionists and officers accountable, but Trump—the individual responsible for inciting violence—is somehow above the law because, as the enablers now reason, consequences will impede unity. Let's simply wash our hands of this debacle, unify and move on.

And if that's what we do—simply move on—how will we prevent this from happening again? How will we convince millions of Americans who truly, honestly believe the election was stolen that they were duped?

Should Those Who Stormed the Capitol Be Harshly Punished?

MAGA diehards will not suddenly retreat or fade into the background. They have been emboldened, and some have already planned additional riots and violent attacks for the coming days and weeks.

We cannot thwart this until Trump and his instigators are removed from office and the enablers muster up the courage to do something they've failed to do these last four years: tell the truth.

Own up to their actions. Take responsibility. Commit to doing better.

If they cannot do this, then the voters who saved our country from fascism will need to do everything they can to fight against disinformation and ensure these enablers never hold office again. That is the only way our democracy will survive.

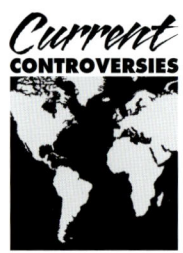

CHAPTER 4

Did the Riot Endanger Democracy?

Overview: Was the Capitol Riot a Coup Attempt?

Clayton Besaw and Matthew Frank

Clayton Besaw and Matthew Frank are affiliated with the One Earth Future Foundation and the Open Nuclear Network, where Besaw is a senior analyst and Frank is an analyst.

Did the United States just have a coup attempt? Supporters of President Donald Trump, following his encouragement, stormed the US Capitol building on Jan. 6, disrupting the certification of Joe Biden's election victory. Waving Trump banners, hundreds of people broke through barricades and smashed windows to enter the building where Congress convenes. One rioter and one police officer died in the clash and several other police officers were hospitalized. Congress went on lockdown.

While violent and shocking, what happened on Jan. 6 wasn't a coup.

This Trumpist insurrection was election violence, much like the election violence that plagues many fragile democracies.

What Is a Coup?

While coups do not have a single definition, researchers who study them—like ourselves—agree on the key attributes of what academics call a "coup event."

Coup experts Jonathan Powell and Clayton Thyne define a coup d'etat as "an overt attempt by the military or other elites within the state apparatus to unseat the sitting head of state using unconstitutional means."

"Was It a Coup? No, but Siege on US Capitol Was the Election Violence of a Fragile Democracy," by Clayton Besaw and Matthew Frank, The Conversation, January 6, 2021. https://theconversation.com/was-it-a-coup-no-but-siege-on-us-capitol-was-the-election-violence-of-a-fragile-democracy-152803. Licensed under CC BY-ND 4.0.

Essentially, three parameters are used to judge whether an insurrection is a coup event:

1. Are the perpetrators agents of the state, such as military officials or rogue governmental officials?
2. Is the target of the insurrection the chief executive of the government?
3. Do the plotters use illegal and unconstitutional methods to seize executive power?

Coups and Coup Attempts

A successful coup occurred in Egypt on July 3, 2013, when army chief Abdel Fattah al-Sisi forcefully removed the country's unpopular president, Mohamed Morsi. Morsi, Egypt's first democratically elected leader, had recently overseen the writing of a new constitution. Al-Sisi suspended that, too. This qualifies as a coup because al-Sisi seized power illegally and introduced his own rule of law in the ashes of the elected government.

Coups don't always succeed in overthrowing the government.

In 2016, members of the Turkish military attempted to remove Turkey's strongman president, Reçep Erdogan, from power. Soldiers seized key areas in Ankara, the capital, and Istanbul, including the Bosphorus Bridge and two airports. But the coup lacked coordination and widespread support, and it failed quickly after President Erdogan called on his supporters to confront the plotters. Erdogan remains in power today.

What Happened at the US Capitol?

The uprising at the Capitol building does not meet all three criteria of a coup.

Trump's rioting supporters targeted a branch of executive authority—Congress—and they did so illegally, through trespassing and property destruction. Categories #2 and #3, check.

As for category #1, the rioters appeared to be civilians operating of their own volition, not state actors. President Trump did incite his followers to march on the Capitol building less than an hour before the crowd invaded the grounds, insisting the election had been stolen and saying "We will not take it anymore." This comes after months of spreading unfounded electoral lies and conspiracies that created a perception of government malfeasance in the mind of many Trump supporters.

Whether the president's motivation in inflaming the anger of his supporters was to assault Congress is not clear, and he tepidly told them to go home as the violence escalated. For now it seems the riot in Washington, D.C., was enacted without the approval, aid or active leadership of government actors like the military, police or sympathetic GOP officials.

American political elites are hardly blameless, though.

By spreading conspiracy theories about election fraud, numerous Republican senators, including Josh Hawley and Ted Cruz, created the conditions for political violence in the United States, and specifically electoral-related violence.

Academics have documented that contentious political rhetoric fuels the risk of election-related violence. Elections are high-stakes; they represent a transfer of political power. When government officials demean and discredit democratic institutions as a simmering political conflict is underway, contested elections can trigger political violence and mob rule.

So What Did Happen?

The shocking events of Jan. 6 were political violence of the sort that too often mars elections in young or unstable democracies.

Bangladeshi elections suffer from perennial mob violence and political insurrections due to years of government violence and opposition anger. Its 2015 and 2018 elections looked more like war zones than democratic transitions.

In Cameroon, armed dissidents perpetrated violence in the 2020 election, targeting government buildings, opposition figures and innocent bystanders alike. Their aim was to delegitimize the vote in response to sectarian violence and government overreach.

The United States' electoral violence differs in cause and context from that seen in Bangladesh and Cameroon, but the action was similar. The US didn't have a coup, but this Trump-encouraged insurrection is likely to send the country down a politically and socially turbulent road.

Most Voters Say the Capitol Riot Threatened Democracy

Matthew Smith, Jamie Ballard, and Linley Sanders

Matthew Smith is YouGov's Head of data journalism, based in the UK. Jamie Ballard is a data journalist for YouGov. Linley Sanders is a data journalist for YouGov.

Supporters of President Donald Trump stormed the US Capitol earlier this afternoon to protest lawmakers certifying Joe Biden's election victory. According to initial reports, one person was shot and killed and at least one explosive device was found in the area.

A YouGov Direct poll of 1,397 registered voters who had heard about the event finds that most (62%) voters perceive these actions as a threat to democracy. Democrats (93%) overwhelmingly see it this way, while most (55%) Independents also agree. Among Republicans, however, only a quarter (27%) think this should be considered a threat to democracy, with two-thirds (68%) saying otherwise.

In fact, many Republicans (45%) actively support the actions of those at the Capitol, although as many expressed their opposition (43%).

Among all voters, almost two-thirds (63%) say that they "strongly" oppose the actions taken by President Trump's supporters, with another 8% say they "somewhat" oppose what has happened.

Overall, one in five voters (21%) say they support the goings-on at the Capitol. Those who believe that voter fraud took place and affected the election outcome are especially likely to feel that today's events were justified, at 56%.

"Most Voters Say the Events at the US Capitol Are a Threat to Democracy," by Matthew Smith, Jamie Ballard, and Linley Sanders, January 7, 2021. Copyright ©2021 by YouGov, Reprinted by permission. Used with permission.

The partisan difference in support could be down to differing perceptions of the nature of the protests. While 59% of voters who are aware of the events at the Capitol perceive them as being more violent than more peaceful (28%), the opposite is true of Republicans. By 58% to 22%, Republicans see the goings on as more peaceful than more violent.

Who Is Responsible for What Is Happening at the Capitol?

Republican Senator Mitt Romney laid the blame for the breach squarely at President Trump's feet, saying "This is what the president has caused today, this insurrection."

Most voters agree. A majority (55%) say that President Trump is "a great deal to blame" for the actions of those who charged the Capitol, with another 11% saying he is "somewhat to blame." About four in ten (42%) also say that the Congressional Republicans who said that they would vote against certifying the election results are "a great deal to blame," and another 20% think they are "somewhat to blame."

Far fewer voters think President-elect Joe Biden is a great deal (17%) or somewhat (9%) to blame. That being said, Biden is the biggest culprit in the eyes of Republicans, at 52%, compared to 28% for Donald Trump and 26% for the Congressional Republicans who opposed certification of the election results.

Democratic lawmakers including Ayanna Pressley and Ilhan Omar have called on Vice President Mike Pence to invoke the 25th Amendment and remove President Trump from office in light of today's events.

Half (50%) of voters agree, saying they think it would be appropriate for Donald Trump to be removed from office immediately because of what happened today. Another 42% believe that such an action would be inappropriate. Republicans (85%) are especially likely to say they believe this would be inappropriate.

Are Those in the Capitol building Extremists, Terrorists or Patriots?

Those on both sides of the dispute are at odds in their descriptions of those currently occupying the US Capitol. NPR tweeted guidance that they would not be referring to them as "protestors," but rather as "pro-Trump extremists," and what they are doing as "insurrection." (In this they are mirroring Romney's assessment of the situation).

About half (52%) of voters agree with the "extremist" label, the most commonly selected of all the terms we put to respondents. Nearly as many (49%) think "domestic terrorists" is an appropriate title, and 41% consider them "criminals."

The president's daughter, Ivanka Trump, tweeted earlier in the day referring to those at the Capitol as "patriots." The tweet has since been deleted. Only about one in seven (15%) agreed with the "patriot" label, although this rises to 30% of Republicans and 40% among those who think there was enough fraud at the election last year to change the outcome.

Methodology

YouGov polled 1,448 registered voters, including 1,397 who were aware of the events at the Capitol. The survey was conducted on January 6, 2021 between 5:17 p.m. and 5:42 p.m. Eastern time. The survey was carried out through YouGov Direct. Data is weighted on age, gender, education level, political affiliation and ethnicity to be nationally representative of adults in the United States. The margin of error is approximately 3.3% for the overall sample.

Young People Worry About the Future of America in the Wake of the Capitol Riot

Artea Brahaj, Hannah J. Martinez, and Meimei Xu

Artea Brahaj, Hannah J. Martinez, and Meimei Xu are staff writers for the Harvard Crimson.

Undergraduates living in Washington, D.C. said they felt shock, frustration, and worry as a mob waving Trump flags violently stormed the Capitol building during the Electoral College vote certification process on Wednesday.

The mob forced members of Congress to evacuate and halted the certification process. The demonstrators gathered to support President Donald J. Trump along with a faction of congressional Republicans that aimed to contest the election results based on debunked claims of voter fraud.

Several students living in D.C. reported staying indoors despite the historical significance of the moment to avoid the ongoing demonstrations during the vote certification process.

"Although it was in a sense something of history in the making, it wasn't necessarily a history we wanted to be too close to, so we stayed put at home," Kira L. Medish '21 said. "But I think for a number of reasons, we were all sitting there for many hours, just watching it. It's kind of like being in a state of shock. You can't really take your eyes away from the screen."

Despite the frequency of protests in D.C., College students living in the area said that the violence of the riot Wednesday afternoon shocked them.

"I kind of expected this to be one of the smaller rallies," Afia S. Tyus '20-'21 said. "The Trump rallies generally get overcrowded by

---

"'So Deeply Wrong': Undergraduates in D.C. React to Capitol Hill Riot," by Artea Brahaj, Hannah J. Martinez, and Meimei Xu, *Harvard Crimson*, January 7, 2021. Reprinted by permission.

Did the Riot Endanger Democracy?

counter-protests, and this is kind of the first that has really gained traction. So this was honestly shocking."

Many students said that they were "upset," "angry," and "disappointed" as the riot went on.

"Somebody [walked] with a Confederate flag through the Capitol building. That is just so deeply wrong," Sophia "Rocket" Claman '21, who is a Crimson Blog editor, said. "This was just an attempt to thwart democracy and refuse to accept election results, and it was a seditious act, and it was spurred on by the President of the United States."

"It's embarrassing. And it's really disappointing and frustrating, and it has made me really, really angry," she added.

Andrew S. Jing '24 said seeing people flood the floors of the House and Senate was "surreal," given the stringent security measures that visitors to the Capitol must adhere to during regular tours of the building.

Jing added that, as a D.C. native, seeing the demonstrations on the Capitol Hill was "really hard."

"It's really hard to imagine if you're not from D.C., but the one thing that I've learned this year is that when the news is close to home, it becomes extremely visceral, and it's in your backyard," Jing said.

A concern among D.C. residents is that many violent demonstrators do not realize the impact their actions have on the surrounding neighborhoods, according to Samantha C. W. O'Sullivan '22. She said the racially-charged rhetoric invoked in these riots have created an unsafe environment for Black families.

"These riots show how so many people view D.C. as a political playground in that they see it as a place they can come and express their frustrations, overwhelmingly Trump supporters," O'Sullivan said. "A lot of people don't see D.C. as a place where people live and have homes and families."

"As a Black American living in D.C., it's scary seeing a city that at least, at one point, had a majority Black population now has people raising Confederate flags and hanging up nooses," she said. "If anything, I hope this highlights a need for D.C. statehood and autonomy because the D.C. mayor and government could not enact anything without congressional approval."

As the rioters descended on the Capitol, D.C. Mayor Muriel Bowser requested a full deployment of the D.C. National Guard, which had to be approved by the Pentagon because D.C. is not a state.

Some Harvard students also reported disparities in the police response to Wednesday's insurrection compared to the Black Lives Matter protests last summer.

Naomi P. Davy '22 said she noticed heavy security personnel during her time protesting for racial justice in D.C.

"I participated in the BLM protests over the summer and I know there was a lot of security there. I saw a military tank down at 16th Street," Davy said. "Yet now I'm watching cops run away from protestors, which is really upsetting because what they're doing can be akin to treason or sedition."

"The most glaring thing about this is the blatant double standard but as a Black woman this is to be expected, there's just more evidence to it these days," she added. "It should be a message to the rest of America that something is wrong when there's less security and outrage for this than protests that say Black lives matter."

Tyus agreed that the police response was "very different."

"There is no way in hell a Black Lives Matter protest would ever have gotten this far. People would have been dead in the streets, and we would have seen it recorded, we would have seen it on screen," she said.

Though Trump released a video on Twitter late in the afternoon telling demonstrators to "go home now," Ben R. Schroeder '24 said Trump's response felt "underhanded."

"He told his supporters to go home in the tone of someone who is contractually obligated to do so, like a sibling who was made to apologize by their parents, and spent most of the video complimenting the rioters," Schroeder said.

He said that many Trump supporters likely interpreted the comments as validating their beliefs.

"What happened is the result of four years of the empowerment of these people and their beliefs," he added.

Some students also commented on what the riot could mean for the protocols surrounding the inauguration of President-elect Joe Biden on Jan. 20.

"I think having so many people be so successful today in the riots means that people will hop in their cars from other states, from as far as they want to come," Tyus said. "I assume that now, in light of everything that has happened today, that [the] inauguration will be even smaller."

Schroeder said he believed the riots would not affect the legitimacy of Biden's transfer of power, but expressed concerns about what such demonstrations meant for American democracy at large.

"I am 100 percent confident Biden will be inaugurated on January 20th," he said. "I have worries about future transitions where it's about the faith the American public has in these institutions that are meant to aid in the peaceful transition of power."

"I worry what that will mean for the future of our democracy," Schroeder added.

World Leaders Were Appalled by the Storming of the US Capitol

Anthony Galloway

Anthony Galloway is foreign affairs and national security correspondent for the Sydney Morning Herald *and the Age.*

Leaders around the world condemned the storming of the United States Capitol by supporters of President Donald Trump on Wednesday, expressing shock at the chaos unfolding in a country they once relied upon for global leadership.

But Australian Prime Minister Scott Morrison stopped short of criticising Mr Trump for inciting the violence, saying "it is not for me to offer commentary on world leaders."

Mr Morrison said the storming of US Congress was "disgraceful", "heartbreaking" and "terribly distressing, terribly concerning."

"I am pleased that the Senate has been able to recommence their proceedings, and we hope for a peaceful and stable transition of government to the new administration elected by the American people," Morrison said.

"This is a difficult time for the United States, clearly, they're a great friend of Australia and they're one of the world's greatest democracies."

Questioned on Mr Trump's incitement of his supporters, Mr Morrison said "it's not for me to offer commentary on other world leaders, I don't do that out of respect for those matters."

"I noted the President's message this morning to tell people to go home peacefully, I hope that that's what they are doing," Mr Morrison said.

Asked about LNP MP George Christensen's promotion of conspiracy theories about the US election result, Morrison said

"'Threat to Democracy': World Leaders Appalled by Storming of US Capitol," by Anthony Galloway, SMH, January 7, 2021. Reprinted by permission.

Did the Riot Endanger Democracy?

"Australia is a free country, there's such a thing as a freedom of speech in this country, and that will continue."

Christensen, who has repeatedly endorsed claims of voter fraud on social media, was last year slapped with a warning from Facebook for misleading claims about "dodgy votes" boosting President-elect Joe Biden.

British Prime Minister Boris Johnson said the scenes in Washington were "disgraceful."

"The United States stands for democracy around the world and it is now vital that there should be a peaceful and orderly transfer of power," he said on Twitter.

Other allies were similarly appalled at what they described as an attack on American democracy, though some said they believed US democratic institutions would withstand the turmoil. Some leaders singled out Trump for harsh criticism.

"Trump and his supporters should finally accept the decision of the American voters and stop trampling on democracy," German Foreign Minister Heiko Maas wrote on Twitter. "From inflammatory words come violent deeds." He added "contempt for democratic institutions has disastrous effects."

Fiji's Prime Minister Frank Bainimarama, who first seized power of the Pacific Island nation in a bloodless military coup in 2006, the country's third coup in six years, before winning two democratic elections, called the protesters actions "an affront to democracies around the globe."

"True and genuine democracy is a precious treasure that no nation should ever take for granted. We are confident the USA will soon close this ugly chapter once and for all," he tweeted.

In Nigeria, which has seen several coups since independence —including one led decades ago by President Muhammadu Buhari, who most recently entered the office via a vote, one of the President's personal assistants Bashir Ahmad tweeted: "The beauty of democracy?" with a shrug emoji.

Chilean President Sebastián Piñera and Colombian President Iván Duque were among those in Latin America who denounced the protesters, but both also said they were confident American democracy and the rule of law would prevail.

Brazilian Supreme Court justice and the head of the country's electoral court, Luis Roberto Barroso tweeted: "In this sad episode in the US, supporters of fascism showed their real face: anti-democratic and aggressive." He said he hoped "American society and institutions react with vigour to this threat to democracy."

Venezuela, which is under US sanctions, said the events in Washington show the US "is suffering what it has generated in other countries with its politics of aggression."

Venezuelan President Nicolás Maduro has survived US-backed opposition efforts to oust him despite accusations of human rights abuses, civil unrest and a humanitarian crisis that has forced millions to flee the oil-rich country.

In Puerto Rico, many people took to social media and joked that the US territory no longer wanted statehood. Independence, they said, looked appealing for the first time in decades.

In fact, it was that pursuit of independence that marked one of the last times the US Congress was stormed violently. Four members of Puerto Rico's Nationalist Party opened fire on the House floor in March 1954, wounding five lawmakers.

European Parliament President David Sassoli, who leads one of the largest legislatures in the world, also denounced the scenes at the Capitol. The European Union has spent four cantankerous years dealing with the Trump administration, and its top officials have repeatedly said they are looking forward to a better relationship under the Biden administration.

Carl Bildt, a former prime minister of Sweden tweeted: "This is insurrection. Nothing less. In Washington."

Canadian Prime Minister Justin Trudeau said his country was "deeply disturbed" by the events in the US, Canada's closest ally and neighbour.

"Violence will never succeed in overruling the will of the people. Democracy in the US must be upheld—and it will be," Trudeau tweeted.

Volkan Bozkir, president of the 193-member United Nations General Assembly, said he was saddened by the developments. But, he tweeted, "I believe that peace & respect for democratic processes will prevail in our host country at this critical time."

American Democracy Has Once Again Survived

Bo Rothstein

Bo Rothstein is a former professor of government and public policy at University of Oxford's Blavatnik School of Government. His books include The Quality of Government: Corruption, Social Trust and Inequality in International Perspective *and* Making Sense of Corruption.

Democracy is a fragile form of government. History has shown democracies can be undermined in several ways. It can happen quickly, as in a coup, but democracies can also erode more slowly, as is now taking place in Poland and Hungary.

Based on research on how democracies have collapsed, political science has highlighted what to be especially wary about. If political leaders do not unequivocally take a stand against political violence, do not respect the democratic rights of their opponents and refrain from promising to respect an election result that goes against them, then democracy is in danger.

During his election campaign and even more during his time as president, Donald Trump undoubtedly violated these three principles. His many false claims that the election was rigged, and that he actually won, his support for his Republican party colleagues' efforts to impede minority turnout and his incitement to the mob that forcibly broke into Congress on January 6th were clear examples.

But despite this, American democracy seems to have survived. The institutions of democracy "stood their ground." Yet we need to analyse what principles and institutions in fact saved the day. Some often taken-for-granted rationalisations can be dismissed.

"What Saved American Democracy?" by Bo Rothstein, Social Europe, January 13, 2021, Copyright © 2021 by Social Europe Publishing & Consulting GmbH. All rights reserved. Used with permission. Reprinted by permission.

Luck on Its Side

It's not that this democratic election as such was decisive. Admittedly, the Democratic challenger, Joe Biden, won but in many of the crucial states his win was extremely narrow. Despite Trump's pathological lying and his many attacks on the basic principles of democracy, he received more than 11 million more votes than in 2016. Apparently, we did not hear a resounding defence of democracy from the American electorate. Democracy had luck on its side this time but, as is well known, luck is an unreliable partner.

Nor did the principle of media freedom save US democracy. Until very recently, Trump has had free access to social media and several important television channels have supported him. And nor did freedom of association turn the trick: Trump has drawn significant support from many non-governmental organisations—think of the National Rifle Association—and the powerful evangelical churches.

Nor can a free party system be said to have rescued democracy, because Trump's constant lies about a manipulated election have been widely supported by many prominent Republican politicians. To this must be added that the Republican Party's efforts to make it difficult for minorities to vote and to manipulate the construction of electoral districts in their favour began long before the Trump era and will in all likelihood continue. Nor, either, did 'free enterprise' make the difference: Trump and his party were flooded with huge amounts of money from big business.

Public Impartiality

Instead, two other, less well-known principles saved US democracy. One is impartiality in the implementation of public policies; the other is knowledge realism.

In terms of impartiality, witness the surprisingly large number of local and state election officials, many of them Republicans, who opposed the repeated attempts from the White House to persuade (and in some cases threaten) them into rejecting election results that did not hand Trump victory. In a now-famous recorded telephone conversation, Trump sought to persuade the person responsible for the counting of votes in Georgia to 'find' the number of votes that would make him the winner in the state.

As you may know, Social Europe is an independent publisher. We aren't backed by a large publishing house or big advertising partners. For the longevity of Social Europe we depend on our loyal readers—we depend on you. You can support us by becoming a Social Europe member for less than 5 Euro per month.

A large number of reports in the US media testify to the election officials' strong will to live up to the principle of impartiality in the counting of votes, regardless of their party affiliation. Political-science research more generally indicates that an impartial and professional election administration is a condition of a functioning democracy.

In addition, the courts in the US, including its Supreme Court—despite those judges to a large extent being appointed on political grounds—refused to comply with Trump's demands to reject the result, because he could not prove any decisive irregularities in vote-counting.

Knowledge Realism

The principle of knowledge realism is about the concept of truth: simply put, it is possible to know whether something is true, rather than this always being determined by power relations or by notions dominant in the culture.

Obviously, the election officials, the judges and, moreover, the journalists who claimed that there were no irregularities in the election (at least not to an extent that might have affected the result) were inspired by a realistic view of the possibility of gaining assured knowledge of what is true and what is not. Their determined dismissal of the Trump administration's allegations of vote-rigging must have been based on the idea that what is true and what is false, in a case like this, can be established by reference to the evidence.

Had the courts and election officials given up on the principles of impartiality and knowledge realism, so as to reject the election result for party-political and/or ideological reasons—or considered that there existed "alternative election results"—American democracy would probably have been beyond rescue.

Strongly Questioned

Yet both these principles—of public impartiality and knowledge realism—are strongly questioned, in general and specifically within parts of the research community. Concerning impartiality, consider the significant strand in economics and political science usually called "public choice." This takes as its starting point that everyone who holds public office only strives to use this to serve their (economic or political) self-interest. In this often-invoked theory Impartiality null and void.

The same holds for the theory of identity politics, which has become widespread in large parts of the humanities. According to this view, a person with a certain identity (ethnic, religious, sexual, cultural, ideological) can never relate impartially to something or someone with another identity.

As for knowledge realism, here too large parts of the humanities but also parts of the social sciences have been infused by relativistic views that go under the name postmodernism. Within this approach, it is generally considered impossible reliably to determine by any methods what is true—what is deemed true being purportedly a product of established power relations or personal and ideological perceptions.

Impartiality in the performance of public tasks and epistemological realism thus constitute the cornerstones of a secure, functioning democracy. It is therefore worrying that significant sections of the academic community have distanced themselves from these fundamental democratic principles.

We Need to Address the Insurrection's Root Causes

Maria J. Stephan

Maria J. Stephan is the coauthor of Why Civil Resistance Works: The Strategic Logic of Nonviolent Conflict, Bolstering Democracy: Lessons Learned and the Path Forward, *and* Is Authoritarianism Staging a Comeback?

Following the Jan. 6 insurrectionary attack on the US Capitol and on the country, the FBI has warned of violent actions being planned in all 50 states and D.C. nationwide next week. Last week's assault, which was incited by Donald Trump, enabled by GOP officials and members of Congress, planned on social media, and buoyed by deeply entrenched white supremacy and Christian nationalism at the heart of our democratic dysfunctionality, were not attacks on any political party or ideology—they were attacks on all of us. The entire country has to be involved in responding to what could become a protracted violent conflict or, quite possibly, an insurgency. At the same time, this crisis, happening in the midst of a devastating pandemic, presents an opportunity to come together and build a country where liberty and justice are enjoyed by all Americans, without exception. It is an opportunity we should seize.

What happens over the next 10 days will set the tone for what happens over the next 10 months and 10 years. In the immediate term, the national response should focus on ensuring accountability and telling the truth about the election, exploiting divisions between those committed to democracy and those willing to destroy it, and preventing further violence from far-right extremist groups like the Proud Boys and QAnon.

"We Need to Prepare for Ongoing Insurrectionary Violence and Address Its Root Causes," by Maria J. Stephan, Waging Nonviolence, January 14, 2021, https://wagingnonviolence.org/2021/01/we-need-to-prepare-for-ongoing-insurrectionary-violence/. Licensed under CC BY 4.0 International.

Longer term efforts require an honest reckoning with the white supremacist roots of our political malaise, addressing the toxic nature of polarization in this country fueled by social media platforms' monetization of hate and division, and building and supporting movements capable of transforming our social, political and economic systems.

First, the politicians and officials who incited and enabled the attacks must be held accountable for their actions. Unless there are real consequences to engaging in illegal, dangerous or recklessly anti-democratic behavior, it will be impossible to reckon with our present and deter future attacks. Trump is a clear and present danger to the United States and should be removed from power and prevented from ever running for federal office again. The NAACP is organizing bipartisan support for Trump's impeachment. Missouri Representative Cori Bush has filed a resolution calling for the expulsion of more than 100 Republican members of the House who voted against certification. Indivisible is mobilizing for the expulsion of members of Congress who supported the insurrection.

There are clear signs that the insurrection is backfiring and GOP enablers are paying a price. We need to learn from and exploit this backfire. Trump's approval rating has plummeted to 33 percent and he was impeached Monday by the US House for the second time. Major companies have suspended political contributions to members of Congress who voted against certifying the result of the election. A pro-Trump candidate for governor of New Jersey abruptly dropped his campaign. Republican Attorneys General who supported the election lawsuit are facing disciplinary complaints and the Republican Attorneys General association is distancing itself from robocalls urging supporters to go to D.C. to "fight" and overturn the election. Facebook and Twitter banned Trump and took down the accounts of over a thousand far-right groups while Google and Apple shut down Parler, a platform favored by extremists.

Mainstream media outlets should be encouraged to report on these fissures, defections, and divestments and explain their significance in defending democracy. Further economic and social pressure should target the media enablers of violence and violent extremism, which have profited immensely from spreading hatred and conspiracy theories. Prominent Evangelical and Catholic religious leaders, priests, and clergy who spread lies about the election being stolen from Trump should be persuaded and pressured to tell the truth and repent.

Faced with heightened risks of violence in Washington, D.C. and across the country this weekend and next week, it is critical to amplify the work of peacebuilders and invest in de-escalation and violence prevention trainings and capacity-building provided by groups like DC Peace Teams, Cure Violence, Nonviolent Peaceforce, Over Zero, and the TRUST Network. Activist groups have rightly assessed that encouraging people to take to the streets to confront Trump supporters and extremists is the wrong move—both for very serious health reasons and because they know that Trump and the far-right are desperate to make this a clash between opposing groups, rather than a one-sided attack on the country.

Many civic groups are promoting alternative plans for action. Indivisible, The Frontline and #ShutDownDC are planning dispersed nonviolent actions across the country and in the capital to demand impeachment and denounce white supremacy. These include banner drops over highways, car caravans and a #DontrentDC campaign calling on those who rent out apartments in D.C. to refrain from doing so from Jan. 17-20, when white supremacists will be back in town. In a clear victory for activists and a further sign of backfire from the violent insurrection, Airbnb has announced that it is cancelling all D.C. reservations.

Despots and extremist groups alike want people to feel afraid and helpless. They need to know that they will not succeed. In the upcoming week, a tactical option beyond telling people to stay home and avoid street confrontations would be to invite every American across the country—regardless of their race, political affiliation, or zip code—to participate in a synchronized act of national unity and democratic solidarity. The tactic of cacerolazo, or the banging of pots and pans in unison, has been used in places like Chile, Brazil, Turkey and elsewhere to unite people around struggles for freedom and justice. In the United States, it was used during the George Floyd protests and in response to the pandemic, as people in New York City and across the country banged pots and pans from their rooftops, balconies and porches to pay homage to the nurses, doctors and other essential works on the frontlines of the Covid response. It was a powerful and emotionally gripping act of togetherness.

What if, sometime between Jan. 17 and 20 (perhaps on Inauguration Day itself), every American were invited to honk horns and bang pots for a full minute, starting at the same time everywhere across the country? This trans-partisan, pro-democracy and pro-peace national action, if promoted by youth, workers, professional groups, business leaders, media outlets, artists and entertainers, would be a powerful, joyful antidote to the angry far-right shouting and violence. It would send a message that "we the people" will not tolerate violence and are committed to each other, our country and our future together.

Over the longer term, dialogue and direct action, nonviolent resistance and peacebuilding, will both be necessary to address deeply rooted violence and injustices in this country. It is telling that last week's mob attack occurred right after the remarkable election in Georgia, a state with the second highest number of lynching in the country, that saw a Black pastor and a Jewish son of immigrants win and flip the US Senate. Years of Black women-led organizing and powerful coalition-building in the state made the victory possible. Similarly last summer, following the murder of George Floyd and enabled by years of Black-led organizing, there were thousands of protests and demonstrations calling for an end to police brutality and systemic racism—the broadest and most persistent movement in US history.

The forces that brought Americans together across political, racial, gender, generational and class divides to confront the legacy of slavery and Jim Crow authoritarianism—and to win improbable electoral victories—are those needed to transform the racist and anti-democratic structures and systems in this country. That includes mobilizing around the passage of state and federal legislation, like H.R. 1 and H.R. 4464 that are necessary to protect voting rights, dismantle systemic barriers to participation in the electoral process and chip away at structural minority-rule entrenchment.

At the same time, building broad-based coalitions and movements necessary to transform social and political systems in a deeply divided society is a huge challenge. While conflict, disagreements and issues-related polarization are normal and necessary, toxic polarization—in which the other side is seen as a monolithic enemy and an existential threat—is dangerous and cripples our ability to solve serious problems. Toxic polarization, which some have referred to as political sectarianism, encourages an extreme simplification of reality and the creation of an "us vs. them" framework where "out-party hate [is] more powerful than in-party love." Making contact with anyone from the other side or making any sort of compromise are seen as a betrayals to your own side. The result is that there are huge incentives to adopting anti-democratic practices and tactics to advance electoral and political goals, ultimately undermining representative democracy.

There is no easy solution to toxic polarization. On the one hand, the rise of far-right extremist groups, backed by a faction of the GOP, is an existential threat to many fellow Americans, notably those who are Black and Brown. Four days after seditionist Sen. Ted Cruz defended Trump's attempted coup and invoked the Compromise of 1877, which effectively disenfranchised African-Americans and created an apartheid system, Confederate flags paraded through the Capitol. Meanwhile, US intelligence agencies have assessed far-right extremist groups as the greatest domestic terrorism threat.

Still, toxic polarization, which affects every aspect of our social and political lives, makes it difficult to collectively confront the structural sources of political sectarianism—like economic inequity and structural racism—and makes violence more likely.

Scholars and experts have recommended many potential interventions to address political sectarianism, ranging from creating awareness campaigns about partisan misperceptions and highlighting areas of agreement on key policy issues (like immigration reform and gun policy), to encouraging and acknowledging positive experiences with neighbors, friends and family who share opposing political viewpoints. They also suggest engaging with opinion leaders to stop the spread of polarizing narratives and encouraging restorative narratives, pressuring social media companies to end the commodification of hate and outrage, and creating incentives for politicians and other elites to decrease sectarian behaviors.

These recommendations highlight the importance of making our analyses and narratives more nuanced, engaging in deep listening, highlighting collaborative problem-solving and civic engagement across partisan divisions, and building powerful coalitions and movements capable of building power and disincentivizing anti-democratic and anti-social policies and practices.

At this time of intersecting crises in the United States, there is a great need for the social justice, democracy and peacebuilding communities in the United States to come together and collaborate based on their comparative strengths. The peacebuilding community's expertise in analyzing the roots of conflict and building inclusive processes, the social justice community's ability to raise urgency and shift power, and the democracy community's laser sharp focus on necessary structural reforms are all needed to move the country along a transformational path. Meanwhile, there are tremendous opportunities to learn from activists, organizers, and peacebuilders around the world who are challenging authoritarianism and building peace with justice in highly-divided societies.

While we face the threat of real violence in the coming days, if we can come together and work to address the roots of our deep divide it is possible to imagine a brighter future. In the words of Martin Luther King Jr., whose life and legacy we celebrate next week, "Only in the darkness can you see the stars."

Despite the Flagrant Assault on the Capitol, the Pillars of Democracy Are Holding

Eileen Flanagan

Eileen Flanagan is the award-winning author of three books, most recently Renewable: One Woman's Search for Simplicity, Faithfulness, and Hope, *the story of how she become a leader of nonviolent direct action.*

On Wednesday, we witnessed an attempted coup in the United States as a rally of pro-Trump militants breached the Capitol building and temporarily stopped a joint session of Congress from counting the presidential votes.

Donald Trump called for the protest, spoke at it and told his supporters to march to the Capitol. Fueled by weeks of his false claims of election fraud, they broke windows, scaled walls and looted House Speaker Nancy Pelosi's office. Amid the chaos, two pipe bombs and a cooler of molotov cocktails were found, along with other weapons. One protester was shot and killed by Capitol police, and three others died, reportedly of medical conditions. Meanwhile, 14 police officers were injured by the rioters.

Choose Democracy was one of many organizations to quickly write to its followers to put these outrageous events in context. Founded this summer to prepare people to resist a potential coup, the whirlwind startup—where I served as trainings coordinator—had long predicted that if defeated at the polls, Donald Trump was unlikely to concede. However, his denial alone would not constitute an illegal power grab. What mattered would be what other people did, especially institutions like the military, police, the business community, government bureaucrats and the many other politicians involved in the electoral process.

"Despite Flagrant Assault on the Capitol, the Pillars of Democracy Are Holding," by Eileen Flanagan, Waging Nonviolence, January 7, 2021, https://wagingnonviolence.org/2021/01/coup-capitol-building-pillars-democracy-holding/. Licensed under CC BY 4.0 International.

As disturbing and dangerous as the coup attempt was, the pillars of our society largely stood and supported democracy. "We always said a coup needs legitimacy to be successful. If the goal of today's seizure of the Capitol was to gain legitimacy, the action backfired spectacularly," we explained in our letter on Wednesday evening. "This coup is not gaining traction or convincing the majority of lawmakers, particularly those required to certify election results."

After fleeing the Capitol, Republican politicians quickly distanced themselves from the violence, even Sen. Ted Cruz, who had moments earlier fueled the flames of sedition by spreading Trump's lies and demanding that Congress delay the vote count. Under fire for his role, Cruz issued a statement calling the attack on the Capitol "a despicable act of terrorism and a shocking assault on our democratic system." Conservative Sen. Tom Cotton tweeted, "Violence and anarchy are unacceptable... This needs to end now."

The Choose Democracy trainings always emphasized the importance of bi-partisan opposition to any coup attempt, and the reason for that swiftly appeared. As an afternoon Politico headline put it, "Trump world pleads with the president to condemn the storming of the Capitol." Alyssa Farah, Trump's former White House communications director, implored Trump, tweeting the truth that many loyalists had been dodging for weeks: "The Election was NOT stolen. We lost." Meanwhile commentators like Piers Morgan called for Trump's resignation, the NAACP demanded impeachment and the National Association of Manufacturers called for Vice President Mike Pence to institute the 25th Amendment, which allows the cabinet and vice president to remove the president from office.

After President-elect Joe Biden made a national speech demanding Trump unequivocally tell protesters to go home, Trump relented, though his video message was mixed at best. He called on his supporters to "peacefully go home" while praising their motives and repeating the lie that the election was stolen.

The swift backlash against the coup attempt could be felt within the Capitol, which police successfully cleared of protesters

Did the Riot Endanger Democracy?

within a few hours. When Congress resumed the divisive vote count at 8 p.m., some of the Republicans who had planned to raise objections relented, moving more quickly to acknowledge Joe Biden's victory than they originally planned. Even Trump ally Sen. Lindsey Graham declared, "enough is enough." In the early hours of Thursday, Pence read the final count, affirming Joe Biden's victory. Trump soon released a statement promising an "orderly transition" on Jan. 20.

While the backlash to the violent coup attempt may have turned the tide on denial of the election results, there were already many signs that the pillars of democracy were holding, despite the flagrant assault on them. Before the riot began on Wednesday, Pence signalled he would not and could not stop certification with a letter to Congress, as Trump had suggested. In recent days, all 10 living former Secretaries of Defense published a strongly-worded op-ed in the Washington Post warning against military involvement in settling the election. In a famously recorded phone call, Georgia's Republican Secretary of State rebuffed Trump's demand to "find" enough votes to change the state's election result.

For weeks, Choose Democracy had been affirming the many local and bi-partisan election officials who were doing their jobs according to the law, sometimes in the face of death threats by Trump supporters. As the vote counting and certification proceeded, it became clear that the kind of national strikes or protests planned for an actual coup did not make sense in this situation, despite the president's outrageous fraud claims and the growing number of supporters who believed them. Instead, the group encouraged anti-coup activists to call their local officials and continue to urge them to uphold the will of the voters, a strategy that began weeks before the election.

This logic held Wednesday afternoon and evening, even as the Choose Democracy letter acknowledged "the emotional weight of this moment" of an actual coup attempt. "Strategically we think this is a last gasp and the risks are huge if we simply tell people to rush into the streets," we wrote. The reasons were simple. It was widely believed that Trump was looking for an excuse to declare martial law, and large anti-Trump protests could provide the pretext, even giving him an excuse to try to delay the inauguration. If any conflict occurred between Trump supporters and opponents, Trump would use that to bolster his own narrative. In fact, the right was already blaming the violence at the Capitol on antifa and other Trump opponents, against all evidence.

"This violent coup attempt appears to be backfiring on its perpetrators, and they seem to be losing both in the electoral process and in the sphere of public opinion," Choose Democracy explained, urging supporters to stay home. "They look out of control. Tonight, the most effective action is to let the coup plotters expose how isolated and unsupported they are. Their actions are doing that."

In fact, the protest at the Capitol had not been very large or well organized by D.C. standards. Similar protests around the country had revealed a movement bigger on bluster than support or strategy.

In addition to the danger of lies and a media echo-chamber that doesn't challenge them, the attempted coup highlighted other serious issues, including the attitude of the police, which seemed shockingly unprepared and relatively unconcerned about the predominantly white mob that got through the barricades with relative ease. Some rioters even appeared to take selfies with the police charged with protecting the Capitol they were occupying. Remarkably few of the rioters were arrested when the Capitol was cleared in a largely nonviolent operation—a sharp contrast to the violent treatment of nonviolent Black Lives Matter protesters this summer. As our Thursday morning follow-up-letter noted, "The side-by-side images of previous Black protesters' treatment versus the overwhelmingly white crowd of Trump supporters is breath-taking. It is an example of how racism plays into policing."

Meanwhile, the role of social media is also coming under fire, as Twitter and Facebook froze Trump's account under charges that they contributed to the violence and chaos by spreading Trump's lies.

Did the Riot Endanger Democracy?

By far the most outstanding question is what will happen between now and Inauguration Day. Trump's promise of a peaceful transition came as calls for his imminent removal grew, with even White House staff reportedly discussing the possibility of invoking the 25th Amendment. By Thursday morning, Choose Democracy was encouraging people to sign the NAACP's petition for impeachment, which could preclude Trump from holding office again, while forcing Congress to take a stand on his treasonous behavior. This could be helpful in convincing at least some of the many Americans who believed his lies while also providing a forum to highlight the complicity of people like Cruz. As our Thursday morning letter noted, "We are glad they decried the violence yesterday. But they planted the seeds. When they talk about a stolen election or non-existent fraud, they are still watering them. We will not forget that."

George Lakey, Choose Democracy's lead trainer, noted in an email to his own followers on Wednesday night that the pillars may ultimately be strengthened by the failed coup attempt. "Trump overplayed his hand. As scary and sad as it is, this is a great last memory for Americans to have of his presidency; it helps inoculate against his leadership in the future."

Organizations to Contact

The editors have compiled the following list of organizations concerned with the issues debated in this book. The descriptions are derived from materials provided by the organizations. All have publications or information available for interested readers. This list was compiled on the date of publication of the present volume; the information provided here may change. Be aware that many organizations take several weeks or longer to respond to inquiries, so allow as much time as possible.

American Enterprise Institute for Public Policy Research (AEI)
1789 Massachusetts Avenue NW
Washington, DC 20036
(202) 862-5800
email: tyler.castle@aei.org
website: www.aei.org

The American Enterprise Institute is a conservative public policy think tank that sponsors original research on the world economy, US foreign policy and international security, and domestic political and social issues. AEI is dedicated to defending human dignity, expanding human potential, and building a freer and safer world. Their scholars and staff advance ideas rooted in their belief in democracy and free enterprise.

The Bipartisan Policy Center
1225 Eye Street NW Suite 1000
Washington, DC 20005
(202) 204-2400
email: bipartisaninfo@bipartisanpolicy.org
website: www.bipartisanpolicy.org

The Bipartisan Policy Center is a Washington, DC–based think tank that actively fosters bipartisanship by combining the best ideas from both parties to promote health, security, and opportunity for all Americans. Their policy solutions are the product of informed deliberations by former elected and appointed officials, business and labor leaders, and academics and advocates who represent both sides of the political spectrum.

Brookings Institute

The Brookings Institution
1775 Massachusetts Avenue NW
Washington, DC 20036
(202) 797-6000
email: communications@brookings.edu
website: www.brookings.edu

The Brookings Institution is a nonprofit public policy organization whose mission is to conduct in-depth research that leads to new ideas for solving problems facing society at the local, national and global level. Brookings brings together more than three hundred leading experts in government and academia from all over the world who provide research, policy recommendations, and analysis on a full range of public policy issues. The research agenda and recommendations of Brookings's experts are rooted in open-minded inquiry and represent diverse points of view.

Cato Institute

1000 Massachusetts Avenue NW
Washington, DC 20001-5403
(202) 842-0200
website: www.cato.org

The Cato Institute is a libertarian public policy research organization, a think tank dedicated to the principles of individual liberty, limited government, free markets, and peace. Its scholars and analysts conduct independent research on a wide range of policy issues.

Center for American Progress
1333 H Street NW, 10th Floor
Washington, DC 20005
(202) 682-1611
website: www.americanprogress.org

The Center for American Progress is a public policy research and advocacy organization which presents a liberal viewpoint on economic and social issues. Their website includes a range of articles on the Capitol riot, including "Facebook Was Key to the Trump Insurrection," and "The United States Could Be in the Early Days of a Domestic Insurgency."

David Horowitz Freedom Center
PO Box 55089
Sherman Oaks, CA 91499-1964
(800) 752-6562
website: www.horowitzfreedomcenter.org

Founded in 1988 by political activist David Horowitz and Peter Collier, the David Horowitz Freedom Center was established with funding from conservative groups. It runs several websites and blogs, including *FrontPage* Magazine, Students for Academic Freedom, and Jihad Watch.

Freedom House
1850 M Street NW, 11th Floor
Washington, DC 20036
(202) 296-5101
email: info@freedomhouse.org
Website: http://freedomhouse.org

Freedom House advocates a US foreign policy that places the promotion of democracy as a priority. Its representatives regularly testify before Congress, provide briefings to high level Administration and State Department officials, and argue the case for freedom at conferences, in op-eds, and through media appearances. Freedom House serves as a leading advocate for policies to advance worldwide democracy.

The Heritage Foundation
214 Massachusetts Ave NE
Washington DC 20002-4999
(800) 546-2843
email: info@heritage.org
website: www.heritage.org

The Heritage Foundation is a conservative think tank whose mission is to formulate and promote conservative public policies based on the principles of free enterprise, limited government, individual freedom, traditional American values, and a strong national defense.

Mises Institute
518 West Magnolia Avenue
Auburn, Alabama 36832-4501
(334) 321-2100
website: www.mises.org

Mises Institute is a think tank for researching and promoting Libertarian viewpoints about subjects such as economics, philosophy, and political economy. Named for the famous Austrian School economist, the Institute's stated mission is to promote "the Misesian tradition of thought through the defense of the market economy, private property, sound money, and peaceful international relations, while opposing government intervention."

National Endowment for Democracy
1025 F Street NW, Suite 800
Washington, DC 20004
(202) 378-9700
email: info@NED.org
website: www.ned.org

Founded in 1983, the National Endowment for Democracy (NED) is a private, nonprofit foundation dedicated to the growth and strengthening of democratic institutions around the world. NED is dedicated to fostering the growth of a wide range of democratic institutions abroad, including political parties, trade unions, free markets, and business organizations, as well as the many elements of a vibrant civil society that ensure human rights, an independent media, and the rule of law.

Bibliography

Books

Conrad Black. *Donald J. Trump: A President Like No Other.* Washington, DC : Regnery Publishing, a division of Salem Media Group, 2018.

Corey L. Brettschneider. *The Oath and the Office: A Guide to the Constitution for Future Presidents.* New York, NY: W.W. Norton & Company, 2019.

Robert Dallek. How Did We Get Here? From Theodore Roosevelt to Donald Trump. New York, NY : HarperCollins Publishers, 2020.

Lawrence Douglas. *Will He Go?: Trump and the Looming Election Meltdown in 2020.* New York, NY: Twelve, Hatchette Book Group 2020.

Masha Gessen. *Surviving Autocracy.* New York, NY: Riverhead Books, 2020.

Newt Gingrich. *Trump and the American Future: Solving the Great Problems of Our Time.* New York, NY : Center Street, an imprint of Hachette Book Group, 2020.

Benjamin C. Hett, *Burning the Reichstag: An Investigation into the Third Reich's Enduring Mystery.* New York, NY: Oxford University Press, 2014.

Sinclair Lewis. *It Can't Happen Here.* London, UK: Penguin Classics, 2017.

David A. Neiwert. *Alt-America: The Rise of the Radical Right in the Age of Trump.* New York, NY: Verso, 2017.

Joe Palazzolo and Michael Rothfeld. *The Fixers: The Bottom-Feeders, Crooked Lawyers, Gossipmongers, and Porn Stars*

Who Created the 45th President. New York, NY: Random House, 2020.

John J. Pitney, Jr. *Un-American: the fake patriotism of Donald J. Trump*. Lanham, MD: Rowman & Littlefield Publishers, 2020.

David Priess. *How to Get Rid of a President: History's Guide to Removing Unpopular, Unable, or Unfit Chief Executives*. New York, NY: Public Affairs, 2019.

Philip Rucker and Carol Leonnig. *A Very Stable Genius: Donald J. Trump's Testing of America*. New York, NY: Penguin Press, 2020.

Gerald F. Seib. *We Should Have Seen It Coming: From Reagan to Trump—A Front-Row Seat to a Political Revolution*. New York, NY: Random House, 2020.

Kevin James Shay. *Operation Chaos: The Trump Coup Attempt and the Campaign to Erode Democracy*. Amazon Digital Publishing, 2020.

Edward Strosser and Michael Prince. *Stupid Wars: A Citizen's Guide to Botched Putsches, Failed Coups, Inane Invasions, and Ridiculous Revolutions*. New York, NY: HarperCollins, 2008.

Periodicals and Internet Sources

Luke Broadwater and Nicholas Fandos, "'A Hit Man Sent Them.' Police at the Capitol Recount the Horrors of Jan. 6 As the Inquiry Begins." *New York Times*, July 27, 2021. https://www.nytimes.com/2021/07/27/us/jan-6-inquiry.html.

Vittorio Bufacchi, "How the US Capitol mob riots have put democracy under attack." *RTÉ: Ireland's National Public Service Media*, January 7, 2021. www.rte.ie.

Bibliography

Josh Gerstein and Kyle Cheney. "Many Capitol rioters unlikely to serve jail time." Politico, March 30, 2021. www.politico.com.

David Greenberg, "Yes, it was Trump's fault. But others are also to blame for the deadly Capitol Hill riot." NJ.com, January 7, 2021. https://www.nj.com. January 14, 2021

Clare Hymes, Cassidy McDonald, and Eleanor Watson, "550 Charged So Far in Capitol Riot Case, While 27 Have Pleaded Guilty." CBS News, July 29, 2021. https://www.cbsnews.com/news/capitol-riot-arrests-latest-2021-07-29/

Mary Clare Jalonick and Lisa Mascaro, "GOP Blocks Capitol Riot Probe, Displaying Loyalty to Trump." Associated Press, May 28, 2021. https://apnews.com/article/michael-pence-donald-trump-capitol-siege-government-and-politics-4798a8617bacf27bbb576a4b805b85d9.

Craig Kafura, "Americans Condemn Capitol Riots; Reject Violence in Politics." Chicago Council on Global Affairs, January 14, 2021.www.thechicagocouncil.org

Bess Levin, "Trump Has Reportedly Been Telling People He's Going to Be President Again by August, Which Would Suggest He's Planning a Coup (Or Has Fully Descended Into Madness)." *Vanity Fair*, June 1, 2021. www.vanityfair.com.

Los Angeles Times Editorial Board, "Editorial: The problem with punishing each and every Capitol rioter 'to the fullest extent of the law." *Los Angeles Times*, January 13, 2021. /www.latimes.com.

Kica Matos, "What the Capitol Riots Mean for the Future of Our Democracy." Vera Institute of Justice, January 13, 2021. www.vera.org.

Yascha Mounk, "After Trump, Is American Democracy Doomed by Populism?" Council on Foreign Relations. January 14, 2021. www.cfr.org

Robert Patrick, "St. Louis lawyer Albert Watkins says Trump's failure to pardon accused Capitol rioters is a 'betrayal.'" *St. Louis Post-Dispatch*, Jan 22, 2021. www.stltoday.com

Raj Persaud, "Commentary: What's behind claims of electoral fraud in US elections." CAN, November 7, 2020. https://www.channelnewsasia.com/

Diane Ravitch, "What Trump Did During the Insurrection." Diane Ravitch's Blog. January 16, 2021. dianeravitch.net.

Rashawn Ray, "What the Capitol insurgency reveals about white supremacy and law enforcement." *Brookings*, January 12, 2021. https://www.brookings.edu.

Dionne Searcey, "For Trump's aggrieved defenders, this impeachment confirms everything." *New York Times*, January 27, 2021. https://www.nytimes.com.

Shayan Sardarizadeh and Jessica Lussenhop, "The 65 days that led to chaos at the Capitol." BBC Monitoring and BBC News Washington, January 10, 2021. https://www.bbc.com.

Index

A
Adida, Ben, 41
agnotology, 83
Alliance for Romanian Unification, 61
Antifa, 56–58, 107, 113, 120, 121, 186
Antonescu, Ioan, 60
Arena, Andy,
Arendt, Hannah, 82
Arizona, voter fraud claims in, 34–35, 42

B
Ballard, Jamie, 161–163 Bannon, Steve, 42, 51
Barr, Bill, 47
Bauer, Robert, 95
Bedke, Scott, 133, 135
Besaw, Clayton, 157–160
Billig, Michael, 51
Blue Marble Jubilee, 71–72
Boal, Iain, 83
Bowser, Muriel E., 104
Brady, Jane, 110–114
Brahaj, Artea, 164–167
Bucur, Maria, 59–61
Bundy, Ammon, 134

C
California, voter fraud claims in, 38

Capitol riot
as election fraud protest, 19–22, 23–35, 36–43, 44–47, 48–66, 67–70, 71–87
how rioters should be punished, 116–121, 122–132, 133–138, 139–143, 144–147, 148–151, 152–155
international perspectives on 168–171
as threat to democracy, 157–160, 161–163, 164–167, 168–171, 172–175, 176–182, 183–187
Trump's role in, 89–93, 94–97, 98–105, 106–109, 110–114
Cârstocea, Raul, 58–59
Chansley, Jacob, 149
Churchwell, Sarah, 64
Clark, Justin, 40
Clinton, Hillary, 53, 73
Comey, James, 71
Conway, Erik, 83
Conway, Kellyanne, 98, 101
Copsey, Nigel, 56–58
Cormier, Ryan, 110–114
Crenshaw, Dan, 46

D
Demons, 67–70
Diamond, Paul, 40
Dostoevsky, Fyodor, 67–70

E
Eco, Umberto, 51
Erfle, Julie, 152–155

F
Farley, Robert, 23–35
fascism, academic explanations of and perspectives on the term, 48–66
Fisher, Samuel, 96
Flanagan, Eileen, 183–187
Frank, Matthew, 157–160

G
Galloway, Anthony, 168–171
Gamard, Sarah, 110–114
Gardell, Mattias, 49–51
Georgia, voter fraud claims in, 29–32
Giuliani, Rudy, 15, 46, 89
Goldwater, Barry, 52
Gore, D'Angelo, 23–35
Graham, Lindsay, 98, 185
Grass Valley Charter School, 71–72
Grayson, Kenneth, 96
Griffin, Roger, 63–65

H
Hemenway, Edward, II, 95
Hitler, Adolf, 49, 55, 58, 59, 64

Hughes, Brian, 62–63

I
impeachment, 16, 94, 95, 97, 99, 110, 111, 127, 128, 139, 140, 141, 142, 144, 149, 177, 178, 184, 187
It's Going Down, 57

J
Jackson, Emanuel, 96
Jackson, Paul Nicholas, 48–66

K
Kohler, Jeremy, 133–138
Kokobobo, Ani, 67–70
Kushner, Jared, 98, 103

L
Lacananian analysis, of Trump supporters, 62–63
Lavric, Soren, 60, 61
Life of a Great Sinner, The, 68
Litt, David, 44–47
Louisiana, voter fraud claims in, 45

M
Martinez, Hannah J., 164–167
Matrix, The, 81
Mayer, David M., 19–22
McCarthy, Kevin, 15, 98, 103
McDaniel, Rona, 38
McDonald, Jessica, 23–35
Megarian, Chris, 148–151
Merchants of Doubt, 83

Index

Michigan, voter fraud claims in, 26–28
Morris, Dick, 46
Mueller, Robert, 73, 74
Murkowski, Lisa, 112
Mussolini, Benito, 49, 51, 55, 58, 64

N

Nechaev, Sergei, 68
Nevada, voter fraud claims in, 38, 40
Newbold, Adam, 148, 149
New Jersey, voter fraud claims in, 45
Newman, Lily Hay, 36–43
Newman, Meredith, 110–114
nihilism, 67–70
Niskanen Center, 139–143
North Carolina, voter fraud claims in, 32–33

O

Obama, Barack, 52, 73, 74–75, 106, 114
Ogoranu, Ioan, 60
Oreskes, Naomi, 83
Organization of the People's Vengeance, 68
Organization for Security and Co-operation (OSCE), 42

P

participatory media, overview of, 78–79
Patrick, Dan, 44

Patriot Prayer, 137
Paxton, Robert, 48
Pelosi, Nancy, 97, 110, 113, 142, 183
Pence, Mike, 15, 56, 92, 96, 100, 102, 110, 140, 142, 162, 184, 185
Pennsylvania, voter fraud claims in, 23–26, 45
Pew Research Center, 122–132
Pezzola, Dominic, 96, 97
Plato's Cave, 81
Pop, Ioan Aurel, 60
Proctor, Robert, 83
Proud Boys, 53, 57, 64, 96, 176,
Putin, Vladimir, 16, 83, 84, 85, 95

Q

QAnon, 47, 57, 65, 71–87, 96, 114, 130–132, 176
QAnon: An Invitation to a Great Awakening, 72
QAnon Anonymous, 77

R

Ravitch, Diane, 98–105
Rector, Kevin, 148–151
Refuse Fascism, 56
Renton, David, 55–56
Richardson, John E., 51
Rieder, Rem, 23–35
Robertson, Lori, 23–35
Romania, 59, 60–61
Rothschild family, 73
Rothstein, Bo, 172–182

199

Russian Internet Research Agency, 79
Ryan, Jenna, 148

S
Sanders, Linley, 161–163
Sanford, Robert, 95
Sasse, Ben, 108
Schiebinger, Londa, 83
Schneider, Marian, 40
Scott, Rick, 46
Seefried, Hunter, 112
Seefried, Kevin, 112
Shackford, Scott, 116–121
Sherman, Amy, 89–93
Sicknick, Brian, 16, 119
Smith, Erika D., 106–109
Smith, Matthew, 161–163
Soros, George, 53, 73
Stanley, Jason, 64
Stephan, Maria J., 176–182
Sunstein, Cass, 74

T
Teitelbaum, Benjamin R., 53–55
Tillman, Zoe, 94–97
Toomey, Pat, 112
Traverso, Enzo, 64
Trump, Donald, impeachment of, 16, 94, 95, 97, 99, 110, 111, 127, 128, 139, 140, 141, 142, 144, 149, 177, 178, 184, 187
Trump, Donald, Jr., 100, 101
Trump, Eric, 99

Trump, Ivanka, 101, 102, 163

U
Uscinski, Joseph,

V
voter fraud claims
  history of in United States, 44–47
  state-by-state overview of 2020 election claims, 23–35

W
Westervelt, Eric, 144–147
Whitmer, Gretchen, 136
Williams, Riley, 97
Wisconsin, voter fraud claims in, 33–34
Wodak, Ruth, 51–53

X
Xu, Meimei, 164–167

Z
Zuckerberg, Mark, 106, 107
Zuckerman, Ethan, 71–87